Jennifer Heard the Growling Again, Steady and Moving Nearer.

"Lee?"

He started walking, pulling her close to his side and keeping his normal pace. "Don't pay any attention to it."

Jennifer nodded. She forced herself to remain calm, listening to the sounds behind her. Her legs wanted to run, and her lungs were taking in the air necessary to run. But she fought the urge.

Behind them on the blacktop she heard the clicking of an animal's claws.

And suddenly she admitted what she had known all along—it wasn't a dog after all.

It was one of *them*, in its wolf form. And it was stalking them . . .

iBooks in the **PRIVATE SCHOOL**™ Series

Most iBooks are available at special quantity discounts for bulk purchases for sales promotions, premiums or fundraising. Special books or book excerpts can also be created to fit specific needs.

For details, email the publisher
@bricktower@aol.com

PRIVATE SCHOOL #2
Academy of Terror

Steven Charles

A BYRON PREISS VISUAL PUBLICATIONS,

INC. BOOK

iBooks for Young Readers
Habent Sua Fata Libelli

iBooks
Manhanset House
Dering Harbor, New York 11965

bricktower@aol.com • www.ibooksinc.com

Library of Congress Cataloging-in-Publication Data
Charles, Steven. Academy of terror.
        (Private School) "A Byron Preiss book."
p. cm.
        [1. Young Adult Fiction—Horror. 2. Young Adult Fiction—Science
Fiction—Alien Contact. 3. Young Adult Fiction—Werewolfs and
Shifters.] I. Lang, Gary, ill. II. Title. III.
Series: Charles, Steven. Private School.

ISBN 978-1-59687-561-6
November 2018

Special thanks to Ron Buehl,
Pat MacDonald, Marjorie Hanlon,
and David M. Harris.
Editor—Ruth Ashby

ACADEMY OF TERROR

Table of Contents

Chapter One

GREEN EYES

Jennifer could see them down at the end of a long dark hallway, like a cat's eyes following every move she made. Yet she couldn't move, couldn't run; her muscles were frozen, and all the will she possessed could not force them to retreat.

Green eyes, watching

And the narrow, slanted eyes came closer, grew brighter as she pressed against a wall, her hands struggling to find a door, a window, anything that would let her out before what belonged to those eyes reached her.

watching

Perspiration, cold and icy, gathered in her hair, slipped in quivering beads down her forehead like the legs of a hundred tiny spiders; her breath grew hot in her lungs, and the faster she inhaled, the hotter the air grew; and she could feel hatred in those eyes, a warning that sooner or later she would be caught.

And when she was, no power on earth would be strong enough to save her.

Green eyes, watching, and growing

Despite the fear she was helpless to control, knowing it was an endless dream gave her an odd sense of calm, and she wasn't surprised, then, when the eyes paused, and grew larger, more slanted still, and the green faded from emerald to a pale mint.

Green eyes.

The eyes of a wolf.

A light went on somewhere overhead.

And she saw it.

It was a wolf, and it was not a wolf—its face and body were covered in thick, dark gray fur, its muzzle long, its gleaming white teeth exposed and sharp. But it walked easily on two legs, exactly like a man. And its voice when it spoke was deep and without menace:

"It's all right, Jennifer, you don't have to be afraid."

It was lying. The creature's lips pulled back in a horrid smile, its arms stretched out to her as if to pat her shoulders, but its eyes had not changed—hating, and waiting, still sending her that warning.

"It's all right, I'm not going to hurt you. Just come over here and let me give you a hug."

She screamed.

The thought of that thing touching her finally broke through her calm, and she screamed loudly and long, until the hallway and the eyes and the voice vanished in an explosion of fire and thunder. The floor disappeared beneath her, and she fell, still screaming, her arms flailing wildly until one of them struck something solid, pain shot up to her elbow, and she woke up.

"Oh no," she whispered and put her hands on her face. "Oh no, that one was bad."

But not so bad as they had been, not nearly so bad as the ones she'd suffered right after the fire.

Blindly, she reached to her right and switched on the nightstand lamp, blinked against the sudden bright light, and took several deep breaths to bring the room back into focus.

Slowly. In and out, until the last of the dream vanished and she knew she was all right.

Moaning slightly at the dull aches in muscles that had been held rigid during the nightmare, she tossed aside the sheet and swung her legs over the side of the mattress. Then she puffed her cheeks and blew out an explosive breath as much for the comforting noise as for the release of her tension. A sudden chill made her shudder, and she looked at the casement window on the other side of the room. It was wide open, a cool breeze rustling the papers on her desk and the pages of an open textbook. She thought about getting up to close it and changed her mind. First, she had to be sure she wasn't still dreaming.

She pushed her long auburn hair away from her face and glanced around the room—the door next to the nightstand, the closet by the door, the alcove in which her chest of drawers and mirror were set, the desk, two old easy chairs, the Sierra Club prints on the painted walls.

Nothing out of place here, she thought in relief; it was still her plain old, good old dormitory room, nothing weird or terrible hiding in the corners and, when she checked, nothing hiding in the closet.

She started to emit a scream but stifled it when she imagined she saw a ghost, and she gave a quick laugh when she realized it was only her reflection in the mirror. She looked at herself, stuck out her tongue and wrinkled her nose, and laughed again, this time because that was the first nightmare she'd had in almost two weeks. A good sign. A very good sign that she was finally leaving the horror behind her.

A tremendous yawn overtook her then, making her jaw pop, and she giggled, stretched, and decided she needed a glass of water before going back to sleep. Quickly tossing a bathrobe over her shoulders, she opened the door and stepped into the silent, green-tiled hallway. She hurried left, down the hall to the shower room, pushed in the door and ran cold water over her hands, scooped a palmful into her mouth, and sighed after swallowing.

A few weeks before she wouldn't have been able to leave her room at night without an army for an escort.

"A definite improvement, kid," she said. She returned to her room, tossed the robe onto an armchair, and dropped onto the bed. There were only a couple of hours before dawn, and she was tempted to stay up and read a little; but she needed the sleep. The fall term was in full swing, and her brain would be like mush if she didn't get some rest.

Yet she hesitated before turning out the light.

All right, she told herself in disgust. All right, go ahead and look if it'll make you feel better.

She rose again and went to the window. Her arms crossed over her chest; her tongue licked at her lips. There was no moon, but the starlight was just strong enough to give her an indication of the size of the wooded hills that ranged in ragged rows behind Thaler Academy, of the forest that came within a hundred yards of the school's main buildings, of the area far to her right behind the other buildings, where the trees had been cleared to make room for playing fields, and a sprawling gymnasium with an enclosed Olympicsized pool in the rear.

And to the left, just over where the night seemed blackest, she couldn't see anything but the dark wall of trees, but she knew there was a clearing back in the woods that once held what she had thought was a deserted building. Only, it wasn't empty; it had once been a place of secret experimentation by . . . she shook her head and turned away.

Even now, she couldn't believe it.

Three people had been involved, and she was the only one who knew they hadn't been human. They were the ones who were the wolves of her nightmares; they were the ones who had killed a fellow student because the girl had stumbled onto their secret laboratory; and they were the ones who had almost killed her and her friends.

But she had beaten them.

And no one else knew what she had really seen. Certainly not her parents—if she ever told them they would think she was working too hard and having a breakdown. She didn't want to be yanked out of school.

The breeze grew cooler, and she reluctantly closed the window, latched it, and returned to the bed.

Are you happy now? she asked herself silently.

She wasn't, but for the time being she had to be satisfied with the knowledge that the building was really gone, the creatures really dead.

Now all she had to do was convince herself that there weren't any more.

Morning came too soon.

One moment she was lying in the dark, staring blindly at the ceiling, and the next thing she knew there was chatter and laughter in the hall, someone pounding on her door to get her up, someone else screaming that if they didn't hurry, *now*, they wouldn't get any breakfast.

She grabbed her towel and robe and ran to the shower room. Luckily, there was an empty stall, and after she yanked the white plastic curtain closed, she shut her eyes against the cold spray, telling herself the punishment her slender figure took was good for her, that it raced the blood and cleared the brain and would, for a while at least, make her reasonably civilized.

"Hey, Field, you drown in there or what?"

"Not yet!"

"Well, hurry up before you do!"

It was Barbara O'Malley, red-haired and freckled and forever on a diet even though she was only slightly chubby and not nearly so huge as she thought she was.

"In a minute," Jennifer called back.

"Another minute and you'll look like a prune! Don't they have any water where you come from?"

"Of course they do, honey," another, deeper voice answered before she could. It was a deliberately lazy Virginia drawl, and it belonged to Marysue Beauford. "Why, they just trot on down to the little old stream and get all the water they want, don't you know that?"

"A prune!" Barbara repeated loudly. "A raisin, for crying out loud! C'mon, Jenny, get the lead out, huh?"

"Oh, my dear," Marysue said, "can't you see the child is communing with Nature? Don't you under-stand—"

Without warning, Jennifer whipped the shower curtain back and yanked up the nozzle. Marysue, who was standing just where she suspected, shrieked when the cold water drenched her deep black hair. O'Malley and several other girls jumped out of the way, laughing too hard to do anything to retaliate.

The curtain fell back into place.

Beauford slammed a hairbrush onto one of the basins lined up along the opposite wall. "Field, that's the second time you've done that. I have half a mind to whip you, girl."

Jennifer laughed, dried herself off, and wrapped her towel around her head. When she came out, most of the others were gone; Marysue, though fully dressed, was grumbling under a towel of her own.

"Sorry about the hair," Jennifer said.

"I'll bet." Marysue, more than anyone Jennifer had met at Thaler, was extremely conscious of her appearance and seldom went out of the dorm less than perfectly groomed, even when she was in jeans and an old shirt. She was, in fact, one of the few who had complained when the academy's dress code had been revised that very term to permit its students to wear whatever they wanted to class and to dinner.

She was also, like most of the others, wealthy. Were it not for a scholarship, Jennifer could never have afforded to come to Thaler.

"Listen," Jennifer asked as they crossed out into the hall, "you going to town tonight?"

"Me?"

"Yes," she said. "You."

"Whatever for?"

Jennifer grinned. "I don't know. A movie. Something to eat at the Hilltop. Conrad Chang."

Marysue stopped and stared at her. "Conrad Chang?"

"Oh? You never heard of him?"

Marysue whipped off the towel and rebrushed her hair. "The name," she said casually, "is awfully familiar."

Jennifer nodded and would have said something more had not a shout in the corridor warned them that the dining hall would be closed in less than twenty minutes. Immediately, she raced back to her room, dressed in a white shirt and jeans, pulled on the western boots she had bought only the week before, and was out and down the stairs almost before she had time to take a breath.

It wasn't until she burst into the dining hall and was in line that she remembered her books. The urge to fetch them had her in a half turn, but the smell of breakfast was too strong. Later, she thought. Her first class wasn't for another thirty minutes, plenty of time to grab something to eat and return to her room to get what she needed.

She went through the line as fast as she could, found a place at a table near the swinging doors in the back, and ate quickly. Too quickly. By the time she had dropped her tray and empty dishes at the cleaning station, her stomach was protesting.

Idiot, she told herself as she rushed back outside; you're an idiot. A jerk. A—

"Hey! Watch where you're going, huh?"

The warning came too late. Not three steps out of the door, and she collided with someone, books and notebooks dropping to the ground. Without seeing who it was, she scrambled around on her hands and knees, snatching up a text here, grabbing a sheet of paper there, until she rose, grinned, and turned to hand it all over.

The grin froze.

"Field, you'd better get your act together, you know what I mean?"

The papers and book were yanked from her hands, and she could only watch mutely as the blond-haired girl strode off toward the classrooms.

It was Monica Holt. Her best friend and guide during the summer session; now she behaved as if she barely knew her.

Jennifer stared after her until Marysue touched her shoulder, and she almost screamed.

"Jen, hey, are you okay?"

Jennifer nodded absently. "Yes," she said softly. "Yes, I think so."

"Well, c'mon then! Get your stuff. I'll wait for you here. No sense in one of us being late when we both can be."

Jennifer smiled briefly and headed for the stairs. It was several days since she had seen Monica, and now, bumping into her that way, she remembered what she knew had to have been a dream, a bad dream.

A dream in which Monica had the green eyes of a wolf.

Chapter Two

THALER ACADEMY STOOD ON A HUNDRED ACRES OF rolling land just outside the small community of Staines in western Connecticut. Entering the campus between two huge marble pillars, a visitor would follow a long curving drive toward an arc of seven red-brick, colonial-style buildings. On the far left was a dormitory; beside it was the Student Union, another dorm, the administration building, two classroom buildings, and the last dorm. Though there was a gap of a dozen yards or more between each set of buildings, they were all connected by roofed walkways that protected the students from most of the rain and some of the sun.

Now, as Jennifer stood in front of the Student Union, *she* wished that the roof also offered some protection against the chill in the air. An autumn chill that was already beginning to turn the leaves to their October colors. She shivered, wondering why she hadn't worn a sweater to her last class, and jumped when someone spoke to her.

Barbara O'Malley stood there and laughed. "Field," she said, "it looks to me like you're thinking. Don't you know that's not allowed? It's Friday, it's"—she looked at her wristwatch and scowled—"it's almost five o'clock, and we don't have to use our brains again until Monday."

"Boy, don't I wish," Jennifer said. "You ought to see the paper I was just assigned."

"Paper?" Barbara gasped. "You mean work? On a weekend? Not going into Staines tonight?"

Jennifer nodded reluctantly. Because she was on a scholarship, she had to maintain grades that would keep the faculty off her back and her parents happy. But she enjoyed studying, enjoyed learning simply to learn new things.

Though it did, on occasion, put a dent in her social life.

At that moment Marysue bustled out of the Union, saw them, and hurried over. "Well?" she said. "Are we ready or what?"

"I'm ready," Barbara said. "But I don't know about Field."

Beauford frowned, looked at O'Malley, and nodded once. Suddenly, amid a burst of laughter, Jennifer found herself being propelled along the walk toward the dorm. She tried to protest, but she couldn't stop giggling, and by the time they were inside she knew Barbara was right. It was one thing to work all week; it was quite another to do it without taking a break now and then.

Besides, she thought as they shoved her into her room and made her swear she'd be ready quickly, it would give her a chance to see Lee.

She stood in front of the mirror and brushed her hair, grinning. Her reflection grinned back at her; she stuck out her tongue.

Lee Fawkes.

He lived in Staines, and they had met when he had taken classes during the summer session in August, a period of concentrated study when Thaler students were able to make up failures or get a head start on the coming year. Selected students from the local high school were permitted to attend a few college-prep classes throughout the year.

They had shared a class and some of their free time, and when the nightmare began they had shared that too.

She liked him. He wasn't movie-star handsome, but slender and sandy-haired, with the sort of good looks that would last a long time.

Yet she was also wary of him because of the temper he was only just learning to control. Lee had a chip on his shoulder because he envied the Thaler girls who had money while he had to work just to help out his folks. It was difficult being with him at times, but when he wasn't angry or feeling sorry for himself, he was awfully nice to have around.

Lately, though, she hadn't seen him much except in the ecology class they took together. His mother had fallen ill shortly after the fall term began and they were both busy with a full schedule of classes so their contact had been reduced.

When they did talk, neither of them mentioned the horror they had been through, neither of them mentioned that Jennifer had saved Lee's life.

Lee hadn't seen the wolves.

A deep chill ran through her then, and she ordered herself to drive back the memories. It was over. It had to be over. She was all right now, and she would probably see Lee that night.

With a smile on her face, she hurried out of her room and was halfway to the stairs before she remembered her coat— New England nights at the beginning of October were chilly. She grabbed it out of the closet and ran down the stairs and into the common room on the first floor. The chairs and couches were filled with girls waiting for friends or playing cards, and in one corner a group was preparing a demonstration against some Thaler rule or other.

It was noisy.

It was a comfort.

And she was almost reluctant to leave when Marysue and Barbara joined her and pulled her out the door.

The sun was nearly gone behind the buildings, leaving behind streaks of gold and rose in the darkening sky. Ahead, across the broad lawn, the pines that hid the high stone wall separating the campus from the road became a dark wall themselves. Jennifer looked up and saw a hawk coasting on the high wind, and she heard an owl calling off in the woodland to her right. Music blared from open windows, and shouts floated on the crisp twilight air from the playing field behind the buildings. And down at the end of the drive several cars roared between the pillars to the highway.

At a word from Marysue, the trio stepped down off the porch and headed for the small parking lot on the far side of the main buildings. Suddenly, with a despairing moan, Barbara began scratching fiercely at her right side.

"What now?" Marysue said impatiently.

"Can't go," Barbara said angrily. "I—" She scratched again and rolled her eyes toward the darkening sky. "Poison ivy. Like you've never seen."

Marysue jumped to one side, hands out and pleading. "Don't touch me! Whatever you do, don't touch me! I catch the stupid stuff just standing in the wind!"

Jennifer laughed and suggested that Barbara come along anyway; they could probably find a lotion at the drugstore in town.

"No. I have stuff in my room, but . . ." Barbara looked apologetically at them and ran back into the dorm.

"Weird," Marysue said as they continued walking. "I always thought she could roll in the stuff and not catch it."

"Guess you were wrong," Jennifer told her. "Maybe she'll catch up later."

Marysue flapped a hand in disgust and angled across the grass. During regular semesters seniors and those juniors with proper averages were permitted to have automobiles on campus. Most of them did—a car was the only way of getting away from books and reminders of classes without having to walk the three miles into town. Marysue used hers as often as she dared without risking a reprimand from the dean, and Jennifer suspected that more often than not her friend went to see Conrad Chang.

The parking lot was almost empty.

White globes atop tall iron posts lighted every corner.

They hurried toward a battered red Thunderbird that had once belonged to Marysue's older brother. She admitted it didn't look like much; she knew she could have afforded something newer and with more flash, but the bullet-shaped car was something special.

Her brother had died in Vietnam, only a week before he was to have come home, and her father hadn't been able to part with the car, not until Marysue was old enough to drive it.

She unlocked the passenger door, ordered Jennifer in, and started around the trunk when she stopped and frowned. Jennifer looked over the roof to see where she was staring.

It was Monica. Her back was to them, and she was talking animatedly with someone neither of them could see.

They exchanged shrugs, then climbed in and buckled up, and waited while Marysue scolded the engine for not starting on the first try.

"Just like a man," she said, punching the dashboard and grinning when the engine caught. "You gotta teach it who's boss."

Jennifer said nothing. As the car moved slowly out of the lot, she looked through the rear window. Monica was gone, and there was no sign of whoever it was she had been talking to. As Jennifer turned toward the front again, her lips parted in a silent sigh. It was confusing, this abrupt change of attitude toward her. One moment they were the best of friends, and the next Monica behaved as if Jennifer was an unidentifiable face in a crowd.

"You know," Marysue said, "I could have brought a chair along for better company."

Jennifer laughed, and the next miles passed in easy silence as the road sloped gently down toward the narrow valley. The shadows deepened as the surrounding hills brought an early evening to the valley floor, and the lack of houses made the area seem as rough and as lovely as it must have been before the first settlers had worked their way in from the coast. Then, at the bottom of the slope, the first houses appeared. They were neither large nor fancy, but were much like Staines itself—a small town with surrounding farmland, a few small factories, a five-block business section, and homes that were old and generally well kept.

Marysue said it gave her the creeps. There weren't enough people, she claimed, to get up a decent baseball game.

Jennifer liked it. It resembled her own hometown, and she felt comfortable, felt safe walking the streets, more herself there than with the wealthy at Thaler.

They came to the Hilltop, a luncheonette next to the town's only movie theater.

Lee was standing in the doorway.

He must have spotted them coming down the road.

He was gesturing to a parking space right in front of him. Marysue pulled over, and he was at the car before Jennifer could open the door.

"Hi," she said shyly.

"Jenny, c'mon, get out," he snapped. "We gotta talk."

She was too startled to protest when he opened the door, took her arm, and nearly yanked her out to the sidewalk.

"Order for me, huh?" Marysue yelled out.

Jennifer scowled, but said nothing as Lee led her quickly into the Hilltop and down the line of high-backed red-leather booths on the righthand wall. A counter ran along the left wall, and nearly every red stool was occupied, every booth filled, with local and Thaler students having their suppers, arranging dates, and swapping gossip while they waited for the movie theater to open for the first show. The noise level was high, and a jukebox at the back seemed to have been set permanently at its loudest volume.

Amazingly, the booth at the back was empty.

Lee slid in at once and waved Jennifer impatiently to the bench seat opposite. He was dressed in black jeans and a worn denim jacket, a dark tartan shirt open at the collar. And just as Jennifer reached for the singlepage menu, a harried waitress walked up to take their order. Jennifer, fairly shouting over the noise, asked for a hamburger special and french fries, waited until Lee made it clear he wasn't thinking about food, and ordered one for him and Marysue too. After the woman left, Lee sat back and closed his eyes.

When a brief shoving match behind them jostled the booth and he didn't move a muscle, Jennifer sighed. For someone who had vital news, he was acting awfully strange, she thought. Or, rather, he was acting just like Lee—his moods more difficult to anticipate or understand than the New England weather.

Finally she tapped his hand. "Lee Fawkes, what's all the fuss that you almost pulled my arm off? I think Marysue figures you're going to drag me into an alley or something."

"He has more taste than that, I hope," Beauford said, sliding into the booth without waiting for an invitation. As she unsnapped her Windbreaker, she smiled at Lee, who hesitated before smiling back. Then she leaned forward, arms folded on the table. "So, is this a conference open to a select portion of the public, or do I have to eat standing up?"

Jennifer waited. She knew he felt uncomfortable around Marysue because she symbolized everything he envied and resented about the private school on the hill—she was beautiful, rich, and independent. She was also outspoken.

At last he shrugged off his jacket. "I don't know," he said. "I don't know if it's anything or not. Maybe I'm just imagining things."

Marysue raised an eyebrow in delighted interest. "Yeah? Well, go on, boy, go on!"

Jennifer, however, wasn't so sure she wanted to hear what he had to say. At his words, she felt a chill walk her spine, and even before he hunched over the narrow table she had a terrible feeling she knew what he was going to say.

"It's them," he said softly.

"Who?" Marysue asked eagerly.

But Jennifer knew, and she felt her heart begin to race.

He was talking about the creatures she and Lee had confronted in the old science building that terrifying night in August. He'd been injured during the fight, but later, when they were out of the hospital and she told him what she had seen, he hadn't laughed or accused her imagination of working overtime. He hadn't come right out and said he believed her, but neither did he tell her she was losing her mind.

Suddenly Marysue leaned back and raised both her hands, palms out. "Oh no, guys. C'mon, not that again."

She had been with Jennifer when the secret laboratory had first been discovered, but she had not been part of the final, dreadful confrontation. And Jennifer hadn't told her all that had happened because she didn't want the girl to pat her hand and smile and tell her that everything was all right, at the same time calling the men in the white coats to take her away.

Marysue didn't know about the wolves. Not yet.

"Look," Beauford said sternly when she saw the pained expression on Jennifer's face. "All that's past, right? You two guys saved the world for democracy from a bunch of mad scientists, and it's over. I don't understand why you just don't let it die."

Lee ignored her. "Jenny," he said, "I've been thinking a lot the last couple of days."

"Too much, if you ask me," Marysue said.

"Marysue, please!" Jennifer said.

Lee ignored the outburst. "I've thought about what you told me you saw, and I've been trying to make sense of it. You know, looking for a reason for the whole thing, the lab and everything. I've been thinking—I've been thinking, Jen, that maybe they all didn't die. I've been thinking maybe there's more of them around."

Chapter Three

JENNIFER TURNED TO STARE BLINDLY AT THE WALL, forcing herself to concentrate on the cracks in the plaster, on the blotches of paint that covered penciled graffiti. She didn't want to hear it. One hand went to the side of her face, feeling suddenly the heat of roaring flames and smelling the stench of acrid smoke.

No, she told herself sharply, the nightmare was done. She was safe now, and all she wanted to worry about was getting the right grades and making her parents happy. It had been bad enough while it was happening; she didn't want to start it up again.

It was over.

She looked back slowly and shook her head.

Lee didn't press her. He just stared.

The waitress returned with their orders, and Jennifer kept her mind a careful blank while she fussed with the catsup and her french fries, passed the salt and the pepper to Marysue, and pulled a napkin out of its dispenser.

"Jenny?"

"Hey, look," Marysue said disgustedly, "will you leave her alone, huh?"

Lee turned on her angrily. "Hey, just shut up, Beauford, okay? You don't know anything, you don't know what you're talking about. If you want to listen, then listen with your lips zipped. Otherwise, you're not helping anything by mouthing off."

"Mouthing off?" Marysue glared at him. "Look who's talking." She snatched up her check and slid out of the booth. "I'll be around, Jen. If you need a lift back, let me know."

And she was gone, pushing roughly through the crowd waiting for an empty space to open up at the counter or at a booth. Jennifer didn't watch her go, and she didn't look at Lee. Instead, she took a bite of her hamburger and had to wash it down quickly with some water when her throat wouldn't swallow.

"That wasn't nice," she said at last.

"Well, for crying out loud, Jenny," Lee snapped. "Didn't you hear her?"

"She doesn't know," she reminded him gently. "She doesn't know it all."

"Yeah, well—" He poked at his french fries before burying them in catsup. "Jenny, do you want to hear the rest or not?"

No, she thought.

But she nodded.

He pushed his plate to one side, and when he began to talk the noise of the Hilltop faded into the background, becoming little more than a buzzing in her ears.

"I got to thinking," he said. "About those three we found in the lab. Like you, I thought it was all over, but I couldn't help it. I couldn't help wondering how they got all that stuff in there without anyone knowing. I mean, it doesn't make sense."

"They could have done it before the summer session," Jennifer said. "There wasn't anyone on campus then. They could have done it at night, and no one would have seen a thing. The place was all boarded up. It would have been easy."

Lee nodded. "Yeah, I thought of that. And then I thought that it looked like an awful lot of work was going on there for just three people. And we don't even know what they were doing."

She had nothing to say. She had come to the same conclusions herself.

"So, I started snooping around."

Her eyes widened. "Snooping around? Where?"

He shrugged and gave her a quick, unexpected grin. "Just around. I wondered, see, if maybe the old dean there, up at the school, if he had something to do with it."

"The old dean?"

"The guy that was there before Dramon," he explained.

For a moment all the voices and music returned in a rush that made her ears ring, and she was confused. Then she recalled leafing through an old Thaler yearbook and finding near the front a photograph of the man Peter Dramon had replaced. Her eyes closed in an effort to remember who he was. When it came, she snapped her fingers. His name was John Innlake, and he'd been replaced before the summer session began.

Her hands gripped the edge of the table.

Then, without warning, Jennifer had the definite feeling someone was watching her. It was silly. With all those people, someone was bound to be looking. But the intuition was stronger than that—there were eyes staring purposely in her direction, and it was an effort for her not to jump to her feet and scan the crowd. Instead, she turned her head slowly as she pushed a french fry into her mouth, smiling automatically at those who smiled at her, tuning out the voices and the music while she looked at each face that came into her sight.

No one.

There was no one watching.

But she felt it so strongly she turned back to Lee and pressed deep into the corner of the booth.

"You okay?" he asked.

"Yes."

He opened his mouth, closed it, and frowned, and Jennifer knew then that he had felt it too.

Someone in the luncheonette was watching them, watching them closely.

On the back wall between the entrances to the restrooms was a large round clock. Jennifer stared at it. The time was just six forty-five, and already there was a slight movement toward the door from those who were going to attend the first show. She noticed none of it. She could only watch the spider-leg second hand crawl slowly around the numbers, taking years to make its steady way back to twelve.

Then Lee reached into his pocket and dropped some crumpled bills next to his plate. "C'mon," he said, holding out his hand as he scooted toward the end of his seat. "We're going for a walk. It's too noisy in here. I can't think."

Quickly she took a last bite of her burger and a drink of water and joined him in pushing through the crowd clamoring for food. There was a wave of whistles and calls, and she forced her expression blank so that she wouldn't blush. Though she suffered it on campus, she still wasn't used to that sort of good-natured kidding, and she hoped Lee wouldn't get angry.

The watcher, whoever it was, and if he was actually there, didn't show himself.

Then, like corks out of a bottle, they popped onto the sidewalk and turned right, side by side without holding hands, passing under the lighted theater marquee, passing the shops and closed offices until they reached the corner. The streetlamps were on. Neon buzzed in a tavern window.

It was dusk, and there were shadows in the doorways.

Jennifer shivered, and Lee held her hand as they ran across the street, walked up another block, and turned left, leaving the shopping district behind them.

Ten minutes later they reached the town park across from the police station. It was a four-block square of thick mown grass and stands of trees in the center of Staines. Its outer border was a wall of high, trimmed hedges, and a number of wide blacktop paths wound lazily through it from each of its four entrances. As soon as they stepped inside, the sound of traffic was muffled, and the air was made cooler by the trees' thick crowns.

Jennifer loved it. It was peaceful, uncrowded, and now that autumn was approaching, it was becoming as colorful as a picture postcard.

At last, in silence, they reached a long redwood bench near the center, in front of a thicket that formed a bordering wall for the path.

Lee sat with a loud grunt, his hands thrust into his jacket pockets. Jennifer sat beside him, slouching so she could rest her head against the back of the bench. They were facing a small field on which a group of young boys were playing touch football. Every so often a lone jogger would trot past.

Above and behind them the leaves whispered and scratched.

A scrap of paper pushed by the gentle wind scuttled across the path and vanished into the grass.

A glance to her right and one to her left—the pathway was like a tunnel now, broken every few dozen yards by falls of white from the lampposts and their globed lights.

A sudden cheer brought her attention back to the field. "All that energy," she said, nodding toward the kids. "It makes me tired just looking at them."

"I went to see him."

She sat up. "Who? Innlake? You went to see Mr. Innlake?"

"Sure."

"But what did you say? What did you do? Oh, Lee . . ." And she ran out of words, could only gape at him until he laughed.

"You look silly with your mouth open like that."

"Don't change the subject. Tell me."

"There's not much to tell. I pretended I was selling magazines—"

"You're kidding!"

"And when he said he didn't want any, I said I recognized him and asked him if he didn't used to be the dean up at Thaler."

"And?"

Lee twisted around to face her. "Jen, he was scared to death. When I asked him again, he slammed the door in my face."

That doesn't mean a thing, she thought. Lee probably came on too strong, that's all. Mr. Innlake probably thought he was a robber or something, or he had work to do and didn't want to be bothered by some kid selling subscriptions.

Though the field was dimly lighted by the lampposts along the walk, it finally grew too dark, and the kids left, laughing, scuffling, glancing toward the couple on the bench and snickering. Then, suddenly, they raced for the nearest exit, their shouts lingering in the chilly air until they were swallowed by the dark.

A dog began barking somewhere far to the left.

It made Jennifer think of wolves, and she didn't object when Lee put his arm around her shoulders.

"What are you saying?" she asked at last. "Do you think he's one of them?"

"I don't know. I don't think so." He paused. "But I think he knows something about them. I'll bet he does, in fact."

"But they're gone."

"Maybe."

"And if he was involved, he's afraid—*if* he's really afraid—because he doesn't want the police to know about it."

Lee agreed that was possible, but why would a man be so afraid when a kid he didn't even know asked him a simple question? It wasn't a secret he used to be dean, so why act so strangely?

"But we don't know him," she said reasonably. "We don't know what he's like. Maybe he's just the nervous type, you know what I mean?"

The dog barked even louder, angrily now, and they both looked up the path, into the dark.

Then Jennifer said, "I know you're thinking we ought to try to talk to him again."

He said nothing.

"I don't want to do it," she said, tucking her chin into her chest and staring at the empty playing field. "But I can't get away from it—you and I are the only ones who know, who really know what was in the lab. And I think you're right. I think there had to be more than three."

Lee made no sign he was surprised. He only grunted.

And now that she was thinking about it again, she couldn't stop—it wasn't over, and she knew it.

All the explanations in the newspapers, all the announcements made by Dean Dramon, all the reasons she herself had come up with had only been weak substitutes for the real answers.

And there weren't enough answers for all the questions she had.

Something moved behind them.

"I wonder," Lee said, "if Dramon was part of it."

She shook her head. The man was more than a little spooky on occasion, a natural target for suspicion. "I doubt it. He didn't become dean until after it was started."

"But he is the dean," he insisted. "I mean, isn't he supposed to know what's going on around the school all the time? That's his job, Jenny, right? How could he not know? It wasn't like it happened a couple of miles away, right? How could he not know? Besides—"

She sat straight up.

"What?" he said, looking back at the shrubs.

"I don't know. I heard—"

A twig snapped.

They both heard the growling, low and deep.

Lee took her arm and stood, pulling her slowly to her feet. "That dog," he whispered.

She stared at the bushes, saw branches trembling, and heard the growling again, steady and moving nearer.

"Lee?"

He started walking, pulling her close to his side and keeping a normal pace. "Don't pay any attention to it."

"But what if it has rabies?" she asked fearfully.

The growling increased.

Lee pointed at the trees. "Can you climb?"

She nodded. She forced herself to remain calm, listening to the sounds behind her, watching ahead as the pathway grew dark, grew light again when they approached the next lamppost, their shadows swinging to the side, then behind them, then in front of them again.

Their footsteps were loud, heels cracking on the blacktop.

The wind picked up and sent swirls of dead leaves rushing around their ankles.

The playing field dropped away into the dark, and the trees closed in to form shifting walls that trapped the light, created echoes.

Her legs wanted to run, and her lungs were taking in the air necessary to run. But she fought the urge.

Behind them, on the blacktop, she heard the clicking of an animal's claws.

And suddenly she admitted what she had known all along—it wasn't the dog at all.

It was one of *them*, in its wolf form, and it was stalking them, to kill them.

Chapter Four

"LEE," JENNIFER WHISPERED. "LEE, IT'S—"

"Yeah," he said tightly.

A glance over her shoulder showed her nothing. The path was empty, nothing but wind-pushed leaves and clots of dead grass from the afternoon's mowing. Nothing but the distant fall of white light.

But she could still hear it, and without thinking she stopped and turned. Lee tried to pull her on, but she shook her head and stared, leaning forward as if that would give her a better view.

Then she pointed, and he gasped at the proof that they were right.

There, just past the last lamppost, in the dark that seemed to have swallowed the park whole, they saw a pair of eyes. Green eyes. Glowing.

Oh no, she thought, and she turned and started to run. It didn't make any difference now whether she was quiet or not; she had to reach the street before the thing caught up with them—and she took Lee's hand and pulled him along, surprised that she was running faster than he.

A dead branch was hurdled without a break in stride.

Behind them the creature broke into a run as well.

They could both hear it growling, almost snarling, and when they glanced back to see how close it was, it passed into the light, and she almost stumbled and fell.

It was a wolf racing effortlessly on its hind legs as if it were a man in costume.

No, Jennifer thought frantically and faced front again, her legs reaching, her arms pumping, her eyes watering from the wind she created as she ran on.

Then something jumped onto the path in front of them.

Something tall and dark, with its arms out to grab them.

Jennifer screamed and swerved to avoid the arms of the figure rushing toward her. Her feet slid on a patch of damp leaves, and she went down hard on her knees, her eyes filling with instant tears as she cried out at the burning that exploded across her palms when her hands went out to stop her fall.

The dark figure moved nearer.

The wind abruptly died.

Lee braced himself for a collision, his face grim as he bunched his hands into fists. She yelled at him not to try it, to run instead, but he didn't listen, and when she scrambled to her feet with the idea of taking hold of him and dragging him after her, the figure suddenly laughed.

Its hands went to its hips, and it bent over, laughing so hard it could barely stay on its feet.

Startled and confused, Jennifer froze, ignoring the stinging of her palms, not believing her eyes, not moving when Lee walked up to it and punched it hard on the shoulder.

Then her vision cleared, and she almost shouted in relief.

It wasn't another of the wolf creatures at all—it was Conrad. Tall, husky, and blond. In a black football jacket and black trousers, with scuffed black running shoes on his feet. When he turned to her, still laughing and trying to catch his breath, she tried to glare at him for the scare he'd given her, but she could only duck her head and hope he hadn't seen the tears she couldn't stop from welling in her eyes.

"Hey," he said, looking from one to the other, his grin disappearing slowly. "Hey, it was a joke! It was a joke."

"Some joke," Lee muttered, walking to Jennifer to put an arm around her waist. "You creep. What do you think you're—"

"Don't yell at him, it was my fault," said a contrite voice from the shadows. And Marysue stepped onto the walk. "We—we were walking and we saw you guys having a race so we thought . . ." She shrugged. "Sorry. Like the man said, it was a joke."

Jennifer brushed a trembling hand over her eyes. Her palms stung when she wiped them on her coat. There was a tear in one knee of her jeans. Her hair hung in damp strands over her brow.

Suddenly she remembered and grabbed Lee's hand, hard. They both looked up the path but saw nothing.

It was empty.

Conrad Chang was clearly sorry but not sure why his two friends should have been so shaken. He followed Lee's gaze and frowned.

"You guys in trouble or something?"

Lee shrugged once, then started back the way they had come. The others followed. Marysue took hold of Conrad's arm and asked what had happened.

"You wouldn't believe it," Jennifer said flatly.

"Oh. That."

"What?" Conrad asked. Once under the light, his face showed more obviously the influence of his Chinese grandfather—slightly slanted eyes, a skin tone not quite Caucasian, and a nose that seemed too small for the rest of his features. He was handsome, and his combined heritage gave him an exotic appearance that made him one of the most popular boys in his school.

He was also, as Marysue had learned, almost comically shy.

When he asked again, Marysue only looked at Jennifer, who did not explain. She was intent on following Lee back to the bench.

"Did I do something wrong?" Conrad asked at last.

"No," Jennifer said, giving him a quick smile. "As a matter of fact, you probably saved our lives."

"Please," Marysue groaned, but she widened her eyes when Jennifer glared at her. "Hey, Field, you're serious!"

"Damn right," she said.

"Would someone *please* tell me what's going on around here?" Conrad begged.

"In a minute," Jennifer said. "Just give us a minute, and we'll tell you everything."

She reached the bench just as Lee thrashed his way out of the bushes, slapping at the branches and pausing to pry loose a thorn that had penetrated his jacket sleeve. With a look at Jennifer, he held out his left hand and opened his fingers.

They looked closely, and Conrad shrugged.

"What is it?"

"Fur," Lee said.

And it was—a large clump of thick gray fur that was shot through with strands of silver.

"What, some kind of dog?"

Lee shook his head and slumped onto the bench. Conrad sat beside him, and Marysue looked from him to Jennifer.

"It isn't over," Jennifer told her simply. "I thought it was. No, I had hoped it was. But it isn't."

And before Conrad could protest again, she explained in a low voice what she, Marysue, and Lee had discovered. Then, with a deep breath and with an encouraging smile from Lee, she told them what had happened the night the building had blown up.

No one interrupted.

"Do you remember," she asked Marysue when she was done, "do you remember what I saw that night, when we first saw the place?"

"I know what you thought you saw," Marysue answered slowly. "I didn't see anything but all that garbage in the lab."

"It was real." Jennifer took a deep breath. "It was real."

Conrad grinned, frowned, and looked at Marysue. "They're not kidding."

"I know," Marysue said. "That's what scares me."

Jennifer stared at the playing field. "It isn't easy to believe," she said softly. "When I was in the hospital, I kept telling myself it was only a rotten nightmare. But when I told Lee, he believed me. Without seeing it, he believed me."

"I saw it tonight," Lee said solemnly. "Even if I had doubts, I don't anymore." He opened his hand again, and they looked at the clump of fur now crushed into a ball.

Conrad picked it up gingerly and held it close to his eyes. He turned it over, pulled it apart carefully, and shook his head. "It's too dark. I can't tell a thing out here."

No one laughed.

Despite Conrad's size and the impression he gave that he was not terribly bright, Jennifer knew he was actually a budding scientist. Though astronomy was his passion— and his goal was to become a space-shuttle pilot and help construct the first space colony— all science fascinated him, and she had seen for herself the incredible makeshift lab he had in his attic. His mother encouraged it to the point of learning as much as she could herself so she could assist him, and his father, before his death, had done the same.

Among his small circle of friends his nickname was Zucco, after the wide-eyed actor who played dozens of mad scientists in horror films made in the 1930s and '40s. Those movies were his hobby, the actor his favorite, and he didn't mind when he was eventually given the man's name.

"So," Lee said loudly, taking the fur back and stuffing it into his pocket. "Now what?"

"Well," Marysue said as she looked into the bushes nervously, "if there's a giant wolf running around here, I'd just as soon not wait for his next invitation."

They agreed readily and hurried toward the exit without speaking. When they reached the sidewalk, Lee suggested they turn away from the business district. Jennifer asked him what was so special about heading away from the lights and safety, and he told her that John Innlake lived only five or six blocks away.

"Innlake?" Conrad said.

Marysue nodded. "Used to be the dean at Thaler." She looked at Lee. "But why? You think he has something to do with it?"

Lee explained what he'd done, and when he was finished she shook her head and grinned. "Boy, you sure you're not CIA or something? Or are you just a little crazy?"

"Crazy," Lee said, and began walking, forcing the others to follow, Jennifer at his side, Conrad and Mary-sue behind.

The high hedge bordering the park cast a deep shadow over the pavement, and the infrequent passage of an automobile only heightened the impression that, despite the houses across the street, they were the only ones left in town.

They soon passed into a section of Staines that contained mostly small brick homes. Many of them were alike, and all were on small plots of land heavily planted with flowers and shrubs. In the dark they looked menacing, the stuff of gingerbread cottages and wicked old witches.

Finally, at a nod from Lee, they knew they had reached the house and huddled under the sagging branches of a fat maple, staring at the lighted front window.

"This is crazy," Marysue said. "What are we going to say?"

"I don't know," said Lee. "But we can't let him go, right? He's got to know *something!*"

"Well, somebody make up their minds really quick," Marysue said, unable to stop her teeth from chattering. "This poor little southern child is freezing her buns off."

Jennifer looked at the house. So ordinary. So small. Yet inside was a man who could possibly tell them what was going on. Suddenly she couldn't stand it anymore. She stepped out from under the tree and headed for the front walk. Marysue whispered loudly for her to come back, but she only pointed at the door and continued walking, watching the window though she saw nothing inside because a pair of white curtains was drawn over the pane.

The door was blank—no window, no knocker.

She pressed the bell, hearing a muffled short version of Westminster chimes when she took her finger away.

"Trick or treat," said Marysue at her back.

No one answered.

She pressed the bell again, hoping to hear someone's footsteps approach.

"I think we've struck out, Field."

She nodded toward the window. "The light's on."

"He went to a movie. He doesn't want to come home to a dark house."

Lee reached for the doorknob, hesitated, then gripped it. Before he could turn it, the door swung open.

"My lord," Marysue whispered. "Field, what are you doing?"

Jennifer was inside. She didn't know why she'd done it, but once the door's barrier was removed, she simply stepped up and in, one hand holding her coat closed at her neck. She stood in a small foyer, a single worn throw rug covering a floor that hadn't been polished in years. To her right was the dining room, and to her left the living room, where the light was burning.

She took a step forward.

"Lee!"

He was at her side immediately.

But it was Marysue who screamed when she saw the body on the floor.

Chapter Five

THE SCREAM WAS MUFFLED WHEN CONRAD QUICKLY put a hand over Beauford's mouth, but it was the only movement any of them made. They could only stand and stare, and feel the silence settle over them like a weight.

The living room was sparsely furnished—only two chairs, a sofa with matching end tables, and a coffee table, all arranged in front of a small fireplace. On the floor was a brown shag carpet, and on the carpet, face down, lay John Innlake.

Marysue whimpered when Conrad removed his hand, and she pressed close to him, her face against his chest, taking deep breaths and closing her eyes tightly.

Jennifer looked to her right, to a short flight of stairs leading to the second floor. The landing above was in shadow, and there was no sign of light beyond. She listened and heard nothing but her own ragged breathing. Then she looked back to the body and swallowed hard before taking a step toward it. Lee's hand instantly went to her arm to hold her back, but she shrugged it off, took a second step in, and stopped.

Innlake had been a short, thin man with a bald pate and a fringe of silver hair. He was wearing a worn blue, silk smoking jacket now twisted violently around his waist, and gripped tightly in his right hand was a red felt-tip pen. When she lowered herself to her knees, she saw that the carpet was darkly stained around the man's head. A closer look, and she could see that the man had not fallen quite face down; his face was turned to the side, and what was visible glistened with blood. What had once been his face was now a pulped mass of raw flesh punctuated by the empty socket that had once held his eye.

She stood again quickly and inhaled several times to keep bile from rising into her mouth. Another swallow, and she looked at the others. "Someone's got to call the police."

"Why don't we just go?" Marysue asked in a small, frightened voice. "We could leave, and no one would ever know we were here."

"No," Conrad said almost sadly. "We can't take the chance one of the neighbors didn't see us. If we left . . ."

He didn't have to finish. The implication was clear enough—if they were spotted, it would be awfully difficult to convince the authorities they hadn't committed the murder themselves. As it was, they knew they were going to be in for a long, harrowing night.

Lee moved then, carefully averting his eyes from the corpse, and looked around the edge of the arched entrance into the hall. He gestured and vanished, and a few moments later they heard him speaking to someone on the telephone. When he returned, his face was pale, and he herded them outside to the narrow stoop.

"They'll be here in a minute," he said. He looked at Conrad. "I talked to Larry."

Jennifer frowned her question.

"Larry Ives," he explained. "Zucco and I know him."

Jennifer didn't ask how. They were suddenly exhausted, and though the warmth of the house was inviting, none of them wanted to go back inside. So they waited, and in less than five minutes a patrol car pulled up to the curb, and behind it was an unmarked car, out of which stepped a stocky bald man in a three-piece suit.

Lee nodded as he hurried down the steps to greet Detective Ives, who, Jennifer thought, looked more like a banker than a policeman. When he came to the stoop and Lee introduced them, she saw that he was far younger than he had appeared at a distance.

"Inside," was all he said when he had all their names, and they returned to the foyer, remaining near the closed door while Ives, two men who had come with him, and a patrolman went into the living room.

"You all right?" Lee whispered when they were alone.

"I'll live," she replied with a brave, false smile.

A bit of color began to return to Beauford's cheeks, and she yanked on Conrad's arm. "Is this your idea of a night in the park, Zucco?"

They all laughed. They had to. The tension they had been struggling with had to be broken either by laughter or tears.

Ives returned a few minutes later, and his two assistants went to search the rest of the ground floor. Then the detective said, "Stay here," and moved cautiously up the stairs.

"Jen," Marysue whispered as soon as the man had gone.

She looked over her shoulder.

"What are we going to tell him?"

She almost said, "The truth, what else?" until the expression on her friend's face made her realize how foolish that would be. Ives would scarcely believe that four teenagers had come to see John Innlake in order to learn what the man knew about an incident that had taken place a month before. And if they were pressed, one of them might blurt out something about the wolves.

And they certainly couldn't claim to be the man's friends. A few questions, and Innlake's friends would put the lie to that in short order.

When she looked at Lee, he shrugged. Conrad was busily examining the old-fashioned wallpaper on the foyer's walls.

"We were selling magazine subscriptions?" Beauford suggested, referring to Lee's earlier deception.

"Four of us?" Lee answered sarcastically.

Another car arrived, and three more men were admitted to the house by the patrolman, who then stepped outside and closed the door behind him. There were voices outside. Neighbors, Jennifer thought. She could hear the man talking to them, softly but firmly, and within minutes the voices faded. Gone from the stoop, but not, she guessed, from the yard or the sidewalk.

Then Ives returned, his coat open, his tie pulled down a bit from his button-down collar. He smiled at them and said, "You'd better come with me, kids. We can talk in here."

"This is a lot better than the station," Ives said a minute later. "You wouldn't like it down there."

He had brought them into what was evidently Innlake's study. It was a crowded and obviously much used room, the walls lined with crammed bookshelves, a desk cluttered with papers and books, two leather armchairs piled high with folders and magazines. The only light was a brass goose-necked lamp on the desk.

After checking the folders, Ives cleared the chairs and waved the girls into them. He leaned against the desk, and the boys stood by the wall, the living room behind them.

"Lee," Ives said then, his voice high and soft, "how do you get yourself into these situations?"

"Luck," Lee said sullenly.

Ives looked at Jennifer and Marysue. "Lee and I," he said, "and old Zucco there, too, we go back a ways. Between them they have made my life so wonderfully interesting that I think I'd move out of town if they weren't around."

Marysue smiled, and Jennifer did as well, gratefully, knowing that he was doing his best to make them feel better, more comfortable. Apparently, he didn't suspect them at all.

"So," he said, rubbing his palms together, "would someone mind telling me what happened here tonight?"

No one spoke.

"Lee?"

But Lee had withdrawn, his hands deep in his pockets, his gaze on the floor.

"Zucco?"

Conrad made a gesture halfway between a shrug and a plea for help and finally lowered his eyes as well.

The detective frowned. "Look, kids, I know you're shook, and that's understandable. But I'm going to have to insist that you come clean with me. This isn't a broken window, Lee. This is murder, and a particularly nasty one too. That man's face was torn up pretty bad. I don't know if that's what killed him, but it sure didn't help."

He waited.

Jennifer wished she was back at the dorm, locked in her room, hiding under the bed.

Another man in a suit looked in and said, "Larry, they want to know if they can take it out now."

Ives looked around the room and nodded.

"Wasn't an animal," the other man said. "Looks like he was strangled too."

Again Ives nodded, and again he waited until they were alone.

"It was my idea," Jennifer said suddenly. She felt the others looking at her, but she did not look back; she kept her gaze on the detective, who gave her encouragement with a faint smile.

"It's silly," she continued softly, panicking because she hadn't the faintest notion of what to say next.

"Perhaps," Ives said gently. "But I have to know."

She pushed her hair away from her face and returned the smile. "I'm new at Thaler, you see. This is my first year. And my friend Monica gave me an old yearbook. I still have it in my room. Well, I saw Mr. Innlake's picture and . . . I don't know. He had been there for so long that I thought . . . I just thought he might be able to tell me more about it."

"About it?" he said, puzzled.

"She's a history freak," Marysue said. "Every time you turn around, she's reading about dead people." She stopped abruptly and put a hand to her mouth. "Oh."

Ives laughed. "It's all right, Miss Beauford."

"Mostly local history," Jennifer said. "I like to know about where I'm staying. I don't get to travel all that much, you see, and so when I get to a place I like, I like to know more, like how it came to be there and all about the people who settled it, stuff like that."

Marysue sat forward on the edge of her chair. "She was always asking questions, you know? About Thaler and who used to own the land, and so we decided to come here, to see Mr. Innlake so she wouldn't drive us so crazy anymore."

Jennifer nodded eagerly, and Conrad agreed.

Then Ives proceeded to ask them questions about the house, inside and out, before they discovered the body. He was pleased to learn they had touched nothing and had called the police within moments of their arrival. And it wasn't more than an hour later that, with a request that they come to the station sometime the next day to make formal statements, he escorted them to the door.

"Do you need lifts?"

"No," Marysue said quickly. "My car's at the Hilltop."

"You don't mean you still eat there?" Ives said to Lee, who only gave him a shrug and hurried down the steps.

"He's upset," Jennifer explained when the man frowned. "I mean, we all are."

"Yes," he said and returned inside.

Jennifer caught up with the others at the sidewalk, and they hurried toward the center of town. Lee walked ahead of them, head down and hands still in his pockets. He hadn't said a word since Ives had asked him his question, and she quickened her step until she caught up, linking her arm with his.

"What?" she asked softly, ignoring the chatter that had broken out behind them.

He shook his head.

"No!" she said, pulling his arm sharply. "After all we've been through tonight, don't you start pulling that stuff with me, Lee Fawkes."

He looked at her angrily.

"I mean it. It isn't fair. And you know it isn't."

He squinted and looked around, finally freed his hand, and pulled something out of his jeans pocket. It was a crumpled sheet of paper, and he thrust it at her.

"What's this?" she asked, unfolding it and trying to see what was on it. The light was too dark, and she gave up. "What is it?"

"I found it on Innlake's desk, in the study, when I used the phone."

She almost stopped. "You what? You *took* something? Suppose Ives finds out you took this, whatever it is. You could be arrested for withholding evidence or something!"

"Just wait a minute," he told her sharply. "Just hang on a minute, all right? I know what I'm doing."

And he would say nothing more until they reached the main street. Then, in the light of the theater's marquee, he handed the paper to Conrad.

"Take a look," was all he said.

Conrad was puzzled, but he did as he was asked, and Jennifer peered around his arm.

The paper was filled with a lot of black dots, some of them connected with broken lines, two of the larger ones, at opposite ends of the paper, circled in red. It looked to her like a child's game. Connect the dots and get a picture of a rabbit.

"What is it?" she asked when Conrad handed the paper back.

Conrad looked at Lee, who only waited.

"Beats me," Conrad said at last. "It's awfully familiar, but I can't put my finger on it."

When he started to hand it back, Lee said no. "I found it on the desk. When I saw the red pen in his hand, I figured it was the last thing he was working on. Someone must have rung the bell, and he went to answer it still carrying the pen."

"So?"

"So take it home, Zucco. Look harder. If anyone can figure it out, you can."

Conrad shrugged and stuffed the paper into his pocket, but Jennifer couldn't help feeling that Lee already had an idea of what the paper meant, and he only wanted Conrad to tell him he was right.

Chapter Six

THE DORM EXPLODED IN A HURRICANE OF SOUND AND excitement. No sooner had Marysue and Jennifer climbed to the second floor than someone asked where they had been. Without hesitating, Marysue told them, with exaggerated gestures and high drama, of the murder and their involvement in the discovery of the body. She repeated it four times, and each time it became more dramatic, more sinister, until, it seemed, the quartet had practically walked into the house during the killing itself.

Jennifer almost shrank from embarrassment.

There were squeals, gasps of disbelief, and shudders that made some of the girls turn on their lights and demand that all the lights in the dorm be switched on at once. When anyone asked what they were doing at the former dean's house, Marysue turned it aside with further descriptions of the body. When someone wanted to know what it was like being arrested, she made it clear they hadn't been, but they were terribly important witnesses.

It took almost an hour for Jennifer to reach her room, and it was an hour after that before she was able to clear everyone out, close the door, and sag wearily onto the bed.

She had to admit that Marysue had effectively stifled any harmful gossip by bringing the subject up herself, but she wished she had been a little more tactful, a little less purple in her narration. Now the story would be all over campus, and she was sure not to get a moment's peace all weekend.

And she needed it.

She needed it badly.

There was no getting out of it, no way to kid herself— that creature had not come after them accidentally. There were others in the park, and none of them had been attacked—the joggers, the strollers, the kids playing football. Yet she and Lee had been singled out.

That creature, whatever and whoever it was, knew who they were.

And, she thought, it wanted them dead.

Dead, she thought.

And they know who I am

She began to tremble and clutched her blanket tightly until it passed; her teeth chattered from an inner cold that made her bones feel brittle. Her vision kept blurring, returning her to the park bench, the satanic look of the monster, the sounds of the chase as if they were occurring in an endless tunnel.

Her eyes closed tightly, and she struggled to remain calm.

Five minutes.

Ten.

They know who I am

The temptation to throw all her clothes into a suitcase and run for home and the arms of her parents became so overwhelming that she found herself on her feet and walking toward the closet. It wasn't until she passed the mirror and saw her reflection that she stopped, shook herself, and sat again, this time in the armchair beside her desk.

They know who I am!

A knock on the door.

They know they know they know

The door opened, and Monica looked around the jamb. "Can I come in?"

She nodded and watched as the girl dropped onto the bed, folding her legs under her as she leaned back against the wall. "You guys had an adventure, huh?"

"Yeah."

"It sounds like you're heroes."

"No, not really. And I sure don't feel like one."

Monica's blond hair had been clipped short, barely covering her ears, and was brushed straight back with just a wisp of hair across the front. Her face and eyes were slightly puffy, as if she hadn't slept in several days. Her hands fluttered in her lap.

"You feeling all right?"

Jennifer nodded. It was awkward. Monica Holt had once been her best friend, and Jennifer was unable to understand what had come between them.

"Field?"

Jennifer bit on her lower lip.

"I, uh, want to apologize."

"For what?"

"For acting like a jerk."

Jennifer sat up slowly. "I kind of noticed you weren't the way you used to be."

"So did Beauford." Monica's grin was one-sided. "She called me some names I think the marines would like to know. It—it took me awhile to get some courage." She sniffed. "You going to throw me out? I wouldn't blame you if you did. Believe me, I know I deserve it."

"You do," she said softly, feeling a tightness grow in her chest. "You do, but I won't."

"Thanks. You're all right, Field. You really are."

Jennifer wanted to hug her, but something held her back—a quick image of glowing green eyes in the hospital, an image she knew had to be a dream, but after this night she couldn't drive it away.

"I figured you were angry with me," she said instead. "Something I said, or did, I don't know." She looked at her hands, glanced out the dark window. "I tried to ask, but you wouldn't talk."

"I know."

"You going to tell me about it?"

Monica pushed at her hair nervously. "Later, okay?"

The door opened again after a useless knock. Marysue burst in and stopped when she saw Monica sitting on the bed.

"It's all right," Jennifer said with a smile at the murderous look on Beauford's face. "We have a truce, ladies. I think the war is over."

They traded glances, and Marysue shrugged, crossed the room, and perched on the low footboard.

"So," she said and let out a heartfelt sigh. She was already out of her clothes and in a fawn and brown bathrobe that looked to Jennifer more like a luxuriant autumn topcoat than something you wore around the house with slippers and a nightgown. "I am beat, to put it mildly. I am absolutely ready to fall down and die. I am—"

"The worst actress in the entire world," Jennifer said with a laugh. She winked at Monica. "You heard all that out there?" When Monica nodded, she laughed again. "Discount about ninety percent of it, okay? Maybe more if you got in on that last version."

"Well, it was traumatic," Marysue said, pouting.

"No kidding. But we didn't practically catch the guy in the act."

"We could have."

"See what I mean?" she said. "By tomorrow, the four of us will have stopped the Russians from invading Staines and taking over the country."

Monica smiled, the first genuine smile she'd shown since she'd come in. "Beauford will never change."

An easy silence fell over them then, until Monica asked timidly what the real story was. Marysue was eager to go into her act again, but Jennifer cut her off with a mock threat to her life and described in a low voice what they had done and seen. She didn't use the local history story because she knew Monica knew her better, but neither did she give the real reason for the visit.

"You know, ladies," Monica said, "you'll probably be in all the papers again."

Jennifer rolled her eyes. "I never thought of that. My folks are going to have cows when they hear. I'll be lucky if they let me stay another day."

"Worry about that when the time comes," Marysue told her. "We'll tell them you're vital to our defense."

"Like Nancy Drew," Monica added.

"Right," Jennifer grumbled. "That's me. The great girl detective. All mysteries solved in forty-eight hours or your money back."

Monica laughed, and in the middle of it she broke into a yawn that made her laugh even harder. She pushed herself off the bed and opened the door. "Well, if you need any help with the clues, let me know, okay? I'm terrific at crossword puzzles."

Marysue groaned. "Wonderful. I can see it now— this will be the headquarters, and we'll have charts all over the room. Diagrams and things."

"Lists of suspects," Jennifer said. "On a blackboard, with little lines connecting everyone."

"Sure!" Monica yawned again, and it was picked up by the others. "The times, the way the guy was lying, the pen, the look on his face, all that good stuff. The great Jennifer Field! Onward!" And she closed the door behind her on a high, shrill laugh.

Jennifer and Marysue looked at each other.

"What got into her?" Beauford asked.

"I don't know. Guilt maybe. She apologized for being a jerk."

"She was more than a jerk."

"I know. She told me what you said."

Marysue put a hand flat on her chest. "It's a lie. I never use language like that. I'm a lady, remember?"

"Sure. Right."

She stood then, and they fell into an embrace.

"I'm scared, Field," Marysue whispered.

"So am I, Beauford."

When they separated, each avoided the other's eyes. And Jennifer leaned against the jamb when Marysue opened the door and started out.

"We're going to have to be careful, you know," she said.

Marysue looked along the corridor, up toward the front, left toward the shower and bathroom. "I know. We can't go anywhere alone. You know that, don't you."

Jenny nodded fearfully. "Yeah, I know. I just hope I can sleep."

"I will, that's for sure." Beauford winked. "I just happen to have a little medicinal brandy in my drawer. If that doesn't put me out, I'll just run into the wall with my head."

She giggled, waved goodnight, and closed the door.

Sighed.

Put a hand over her mouth to cover a yawn and changed into her nightclothes. Then she realized she had to use the bathroom and found herself standing afraid at the door, unable to open it, unable to bring herself to go out into the hall.

You're being silly, she told herself.

But she picked up her hairbrush, hefted it, and virtually ran all the way there, all the way back, wishing when she was finally in bed and the door locked that there was some way she could board up the windows as well. It didn't matter that she was on the second floor. She just knew she wasn't going to be able to sleep that night, not when the moon looked so easily in at her.

And as soon as she thought it, she felt herself growing drowsy, felt the room begin to slip away. She wanted to fight it, wanted to hold off against the nightmares that were sure to come later, but she was drained, and she slept. When she woke the next morning she was so surprised she lay there for almost fifteen minutes before tossing the light blanket aside and sitting up.

She smiled.

She delighted in the shiver when her feet touched the cold floor.

She stretched, did a few exercises, and went to take her morning shower. There were others in the dozen stalls, and she grinned as she heard them singing, arguing, telling jokes and comparing boys they had known.

And when she stepped out and folded a towel around her hair and one around her chest, she saw Monica at one of the basins, brushing her teeth. They exchanged grins, winced at an off-key song floating over the falling water. Jennifer performed what her father always called morning ablutions, and when she was finished she saw Monica scratching her right side.

"You have poison ivy too?" she asked.

Monica looked startled. "Poison ivy?"

She pointed to the girl's side. "Yeah. Barbara has it too. It was so bad she couldn't go out with us last night."

"Oh, right," Monica said. "Right. Real dumb. It used to cover me when I was a kid."

Then another girl stumbled into Monica, knocking her towel to the floor. Monica yelled, pushed the girl away, and snatched the towel up.

But not before Jennifer saw a curious large patch taped to the girl's side. It was at least four inches square, and it was blood red.

Chapter Seven

THE ENTIRE SECOND FLOOR OF THE STUDENT UNION building was given over to the campus library. There was no fiction here, only reference and nonfiction books that filled dozens of stacks that reached to the high ceiling. The aisles between the stacks were lighted by hooded fluorescent strips that cast more shadow than light, and the windows did little more than add shadows of their own. In the center was a large cleared area for a number of long, blond-wood tables, and on most weekdays every seat was taken.

But this was late Saturday morning, and aside from the student librarian, Jennifer was the only person in the room.

Several books were scattered around her, open or with places marked in them with strips of paper she had trn from her notebook. She was writing rapidly, working on a paper she had to hand in Monday afternoon. Later, after meeting Marysue for the trip down to the police station to make their formal statement, she would take her notes to her room and haul out the portable typewriter from under the bed. She was not the best typist in the world, and she figured it would take her at least two hours to get the work done in the form her instructor demanded.

The librarian's desk was up at the front, by the entrance, and every time the girl made a noise— dropped a pencil, cleared her throat—Jennifer jumped and stared wildly around her. It would take another five minutes before she calmed down and could look at the pages without wondering what the words said.

After breakfast she had told herself that work was the only thing that would keep her from seeing Innlake's body, seeing the creature pursue her through the park— and for the first hour it had been effective. Concentrating on the political schemes of Queen Elizabeth I had kept her mind effectively blank. Until she came across a reference to one of the queen's rivals sailing to France to deal secretly with England's enemy, and also to participate in a wolf hunt.

"No," she whispered and threw her pencil on the table.

It wasn't working anymore.

She looked helplessly at the books and finally closed them after looking at her watch. Time to meet Marysue. She stuffed her notebook and her pencils into a canvas tote bag, returned the references to their places in the stacks, and headed for the exit. Just as she reached the door, the chubby girl behind the horseshoeshaped desk whipped off her glasses and called her name.

Jennifer turned.

"Hey, Field, would you mind giving this to Monica Holt? She left it here last week. Deliberately, I think."

The envelope was familiar—pink, meaning a list of overdue books.

"I don't know where she is, Es," Jennifer said. "I haven't seen her all day."

"Oh." Esther Fine lowered her hand slowly, her round face twisted in distress.

Jennifer almost grinned. The girl had obviously been given all the dirty work by the regular librarian, and Jennifer knew the tongue lashing that would come Esther's way if it wasn't done.

"All right," she said. "I'll drop it in her room, okay?"

Esther's relief was almost laughable, and Jennifer winked at her as she shoved the envelope into her bag and left.

The day was almost summer warm, and she stood for a moment in front of the Union and wondered how things could look so perfectly normal when they were not normal at all.

There were groups of girls walking across the lawn, many in short sleeves and jogging shorts. From the playing field behind the main buildings she could hear shouts from a game, and she knew if she walked back there she would see some of the students lying on blankets, trying to fend off the fading of their summer tans.

There was music.

There was laughter.

Cars came and went—kids going shopping, going for rides, and some lucky enough to be heading home for the weekend.

Normal, or so it seemed.

Jennifer looked at her watch then and saw that she only had a few minutes before she was to meet Marysue in the parking lot. They had to go into town to the police station and make their formal statements. She didn't want to do it, didn't want to be reminded of what she had seen, but there was no way around it. So she hurried back to her room, dumped the bag onto the bed, and angrily tied her hair back into a ponytail to at least give the illusion she felt cooler than she was.

Then she grabbed the pink envelope from her bag and hurried along the hall to Monica's room. She knocked, listened, knocked again, and sighed. She turned the doorknob, opened the door, and poked her head in.

"Monica?"

The room, identical to hers, was empty, and she dropped the message on Holt's desk. As she did, she was reminded that Monica was not, to put it mildly, the world's best housekeeper—wrinkled clothes were scattered on the unmade bed, loose papers and more clothes were piled on the desk, and as she hurried out again Jennifer saw more makeup tumbled on the chest of drawers than belonged, she was sure, to any ten Hollywood stars.

As she was about to leave, however, she noticed something on the chest that made her stop. Practically hidden behind all the bottles and vials and tubes and compacts was the featureless plastic form of a human head. A wig stand. With a brief frown she tried to recall if Monica had ever said anything about wearing a wig. She giggled. This, she thought, was classic; Monica Holt wasn't wearing her own hair.

The temptation to pick up one of the eyeliners and draw a silly face on the form made her laugh again, but she resisted. Monica would be annoyed enough that she'd come into the room uninvited; she didn't want to add fuel to the fire.

With the door shut behind her, she shook her head slowly. How anyone could live like that she didn't know. She wasn't a neatness fanatic, but a mess like that was absolutely beyond her. Monica was probably used to having a maid pick up after her, a luxury Jennifer didn't think she'd ever enjoy.

Once outside again, she moved hurriedly to the parking lot and saw Marysue sitting impatiently on the Thunderbird's hood.

"Sorry," Jennifer said as she scrambled into her seat, but Marysue didn't say anything. Instead, she drove as if she were participating in a race, and it wasn't until they were halfway to Staines that she looked over.

Marysue was pale, and her hair was barely combed. "I don't like this," she said, her voice trembling slightly.

"Neither do I, but what can we do? The man said—"

"I don't mean that. I mean . . . everything. I didn't sleep a wink last night, Jenny, not a wink. Lord, I must look like I died."

"Not quite."

"Close enough." The road swung to the left, back to the right, and Staines spread out before them. "Jenny, I think I want to go home."

"What?" Jennifer twisted in her seat to stare at her. "What are you talking about?"

"Home," Marysue repeated. "I want to go home. Where it's safe." Her hands gripped the steering wheel so tightly her knuckles were white. "Everyone knows, you know. I mean, that I was with you last night. Everyone knows. Whoever's after you is going to be after me, and I don't think I want to end up like Mr. Innlake."

Jennifer chewed thoughtfully on her lower lip. "We don't know that what happened in the park and what happened to the dean are connected."

"We can't prove it," Marysue said. "But we know it."

Jennifer slumped back, looking straight ahead as they entered town and drove slowly along the main street. "So what are you saying? We should all run away?"

"We'll live."

"You and me, maybe, but what about Lee and Conrad? This is their home. Where else can they go?"

Marysue shook her head helplessly.

"Besides," Jennifer said softly, "I don't want to run."

Marysue looked at Jennifer with her mouth open, but nothing came out but a gagging sound. Then Jennifer pointed to the new brick and marble building ahead on the right and across from the park. They were at the police station, and the Thunderbird pulled into a small parking lot behind it.

Once they were out, Marysue took her arm. "Jenny, what did you mean, you don't want to run?"

"Later," she said. "Let's get this over with first."

And it wasn't as much of an ordeal as she had feared. The desk sergeant made a quick call, then directed them to an office on the second floor where Detective Ives was waiting with a stenographer. Step by step, he took them through their evening, to the moment Lee called the police. While they waited for the statements to be typed up, he chatted about the weather, about the film that was playing in town, about everything but the murder.

Marysue said very little; Jennifer held up her end of the conversation as best she could and hoped the detective would think her nervousness came from being in a police station.

Then the papers came, they were signed, and Ives walked them out to the car.

Once they were in, he leaned over and put his hand on the passenger door. For a long moment he said nothing.

Then: "When you girls are ready to tell me everything, give me a call, okay?"

"Oh lord," Marysue groaned once the station was behind them. "What are we going to do now?"

"Nothing," Jennifer said.

"Nothing? But we can't just do nothing!"

Jennifer waited until Staines was out of sight, then pointed to a clearing on the side of the road. Marysue pulled over, turned off the ignition, and laid her arms across the wheel, putting her head on them.

Jennifer cleared her throat, reached out, and touched the girl's shoulder. "There's nothing we can do, Marysue. We can't tell him about the thing we saw, because he won't believe us. Would you? Hey, Marysue, did you know a werewolf chased us the other night? Would you believe a story like that?"

Marysue groaned again. "But I do, don't you see? That's the trouble—I do!"

"Because you know me. Because you know what happened at Thaler in August. But Ives doesn't."

She fell silent.

The engine ticked as it cooled down.

Somewhere back in the woods a squirrel scolded.

"I want to go home," Marysue said at last, quietly.

"I think I do too, but I'm not running."

"Why? I don't get it! Why—"

Jennifer took hold of her arm again and held it until she sat away from the steering wheel, until Marysue was looking at her, her eyes filling with frightened tears. For a single long second she wondered why she was saying all this, why she just didn't have Marysue drive them back to the school, get their clothes, and take off.

"Because," she said at last. "Because something is out there that you and I both know isn't human. I thought they were all dead. They're not. And if there's one more, maybe there're two or three more. It really doesn't make any difference, because they know who I am, and they know that I know they exist."

She took a deep breath, and all her conflicting fears and thoughts fell into place at last.

"If I run home, they'll find me. If you run . . ."

Marysue held up a hand to stop her, fumbled for tissues from her purse, wiped her eyes, blew her nose, and slapped at the steering wheel. "It isn't fair."

"I know."

"I don't want to end up like Dean Innlake."

"We're not," she said sternly. "You can't think like that, Marysue. We are not going to die!"

"How do you know? How do you know some werewolf isn't out there now, in the trees, just waiting to—"

"Because it isn't a werewolf."

Marysue frowned at her. "I'm an idiot for asking, but how do you know that?"

"Because I saw them, remember? I saw them in human form, and I saw them in that . . . other form. When I think about it, I know they're not really wolves at all. They resemble wolves, but there are differences. And they don't change from one to the other like we see in the movies. The human part . . . I think it's a disguise."

Marysue started to laugh, cut herself off, and started the engine instead. When Jennifer tried to explain further, she was silenced by an angry glare.

And once they were on campus and out of the car, Marysue said, "I heard what you said, Field, but I'm going home anyway. And nothing you can say is going to stop me."

Jennifer didn't try.

She stood by the car and watched her friend race across the lawn toward the dorm, her hair lashing her shoulders, not even stopping when she lost a loafer in the grass. Several minutes later, as Jennifer went to the dorm herself, she retrieved the shoe and thumped it against her leg as she climbed onto the porch. She was frightened. Very frightened indeed, but she also knew that running away wasn't going to save anyone else who got in those creatures' way.

Like Lee or Conrad.

She pushed the door open and looked at the steps leading up to the second floor, looked right into the empty study room, left into the empty common room. She took a halting step in each direction, then scolded herself sharply. Wandering wasn't going to help. She needed a plan, something to guide her, until she had gathered all the facts she could. Then, and only then, would she be able to call in help.

The outside door opened and shut behind her.

A hand grabbed her shoulder and spun her around.

Monica stood there, and her face was dark with rage. "Field, who the hell gave you permission to go into my room?"

Chapter Eight

Jennifer, too startled by Monica's anger to say anything, backed toward the staircase, fearful the girl was actually going to hit her.

"Field, I asked you a question! Where do you get off snooping around my room?"

"I wasn't snooping," she said, bumping into the newel post and reaching around it to keep her balance. "And who told you I was there anyway?"

"So! You admit it!"

"For pete's sake, I never denied it," she said, hearing her voice grow shrill and telling herself that losing her temper wasn't going to stop Monica from yelling. "I was only doing a favor for Esther, that's all."

"Esther?" Monica said the name in a sneer. "Esther the librarian? Esther the creep?"

Calm, Jennifer thought. Calm, stay calm.

"She had a message for you. A fine list for your library books. It was in an envelope, and I put the envelope on your desk, okay? Is that such a big deal?"

Monica stood there breathing heavily, her hands in fists at her sides. Then she stalked past, shoving Jennifer to one side. Jennifer's arm went out automatically to fend her off, and Monica was pushed just enough off-balance to fall against the banister.

"Monica, hey, I'm sorry," she said when she saw the pain twist the girl's face. "It was—"

"Forget it," Holt said, gripping her right side tightly and struggling for breath. "Just stay out of my room, Field," she muttered as she went by. "That's my place, and no one goes in without my permission."

"Hey, don't worry," Jennifer called after her. "I wouldn't go in there again if you invited me!"

She swallowed hard several times and leaned against the post as astonishment and anger finally gave way to confusion. What was the matter with that girl? One minute she's all apologies and sweet, and the next she's acting as if she's the queen of England.

And what had she done to herself that she hurt like that?

She wanted to shout something else, but Monica was already gone. With a frustrated slap on her thigh, Jennifer spun around and stomped into the common room, threw herself onto one of the couches, and glared out the front window, wishing the world would stop behaving so insanely.

Werewolves that weren't werewolves, friends who weren't friends, police who suspected she was holding something back—it was enough to make her cry. Only she wasn't going to cry. That was the easy way out. What she needed was a plan, a series of steps that would even-tually tell her what she wanted to know.

And the questions: Who were these wolf things? What were they? Where did they come from?

She put her hands to her face and covered her eyes, knowing that if she were seeing something like this in the movies, she'd be screaming at the stupid girl to stop being a jerk and get a million miles away from where the threat was.

Except this wasn't the movies.

This was real, and she was the girl, and she hadn't been lying when she'd said to Marysue that running away wasn't going to keep her safe.

Her eyes closed slowly, and she made an attempt to recall everything she knew about these things, and sighed when she realized she didn't know much at all. Except that they weren't human, and that they had constructed a laboratory whose location and purpose had been such an important secret that they had killed to prevent anyone from learning about it.

Jennifer's mind began to race again, and she had to remind herself to take it one step at a time. One question at a time. Otherwise, she'd end up as terrified as Marysue; otherwise, she'd make a mistake, one that would kill her.

Slowly she eased forward until she was sitting on the edge of the cushion. A stray hair was shoved away from her face. Her hands were clasped loosely on her knees, and her feet were planted firmly on the floor.

One step at a time.

I'm scared, she told herself. I've never been this scared.

And she nodded. As long as she knew she was scared, she wouldn't do anything stupid. That's what her father always told her—those who thought themselves brave didn't really know what courage was, and those who knew fear and acted anyway were the ones who usually survived in the end.

Dad, she thought then with a lopsided grin, that's easier said than done.

One step.

One question.

But which one? She laughed aloud. No fair, Jen, that's another question.

She stood up before she knew what she was doing. The right question, for now, had just come to her, and she hoped she knew where she might be able to find the answer.

Quickly she headed for the door and was about to push it open when she heard footsteps on the stairs. Her spine became rigid and her right hand became a fist. If it was Monica, she would ignore her, pretend she was a ghost, and look right through her.

"Hey, Field."

She turned and smiled. "Hey, Beauford."

Marysue was still in her jeans and T-shirt. "You going somewhere?"

"Are you?"

Marysue shook her head sheepishly. "No. Not yet."

"You want to help?"

"What are you going to do, build a wolf trap?"

Jennifer shook her head. "Not quite. But I have an idea."

Marysue paused, half turned to head back up the stairs, and changed her mind. "You remember, of course," she said glumly, "that having an idea is what got us into trouble in the first place."

Jennifer shrugged. "This one's even better."

"Great. Just great. So where are we going?"

"You'll love it. It's your favorite place in the whole world."

"Fort Knox and all that gold."

"Close. The library."

"In case you didn't know, this is not like Fort Knox at all," Marysue complained as they took the stairs two at a time up to the library.

"But if we're lucky, we'll find some gold."

Marysue doubted it and said so several times as they pushed through the door and were stopped by a wail at the reception desk.

"Oh, c'mon guys, give me a break, huh?" Esther Fine said in a whine. She was standing at her chair, purse in one hand, a ring of keys in the other. "I was just getting out of here."

"That's okay with me," said Marysue, but Jennifer grabbed her arm to keep her from leaving.

"Es, there's something I really have to do."

Esther walked around the desk and said, "But it is now three o'clock, and the library is closing early today."

"Oh, please, Es," Jennifer said. "Please? Just a few minutes."

Esther looked from one to the other and shook her head. "Sorry. I have a date."

"Wonderful!" Marysue exclaimed and snatched the key ring from her hand. "So go on your date. We'll lock up when we're finished."

"I can't do that!"

"Of course you can, dear," Marysue said, edging the girl firmly toward the doors. "What's the big deal anyway? We switch off the lights, we lock up, and we deliver the keys personally to your room. Mrs. Klopher will never know from these lips that you did this for us."

"But—"

"My dear," Marysue interrupted. "We are upper classmen. We can be trusted." And before the girl could argue, she was nudged out the door.

"Freshmen," Marysue muttered. "They ain't human, you know? They really ain't human."

Jennifer, however, was already making her way toward the back corner, trying not to listen to her footsteps in the large, empty room. The shades had all been drawn, and except for the overhead lights the room was in virtual darkness.

She forced herself not to scream when Marysue came up behind her and put a hand on her shoulder.

"What?" Beauford asked. "C'mon, what's this gold we're looking for?"

As quickly as she could, Jennifer explained that if all the events of the past month were connected, there had to be more than one thread, more than just the wolf creatures involved.

That thread had to be Thaler Academy.

And in this library somewhere, there had to be a book, a forgotten book, perhaps, that would give them the academy's history and maybe the clue they needed. She had checked quickly the past August but hoped she had missed something.

Marysue wasn't sure, but she volunteered to check the card catalog while Jennifer scanned the titles in the local history section. There weren't many volumes— most of them dealt with Connecticut's history, and two were about the settling of Staines Valley. When she checked them, however, she found no mention of Thaler and replaced them with a sigh. She looked again over the three short shelves that should have held what she was looking for, but they didn't. So she grabbed as many books as she could hold from the first shelf, sat cross-legged on the floor, and started skimming every chapter that might give her a hint about where to look next.

Ten minutes later Marysue joined her.

An hour later they were nearly finished, and all they had to show for their efforts were hands and clothes coated with dust.

"Nice try," Marysue said, grunting as she shoved the last books into place. "Good old Sherlock Holmes couldn't have done better, if I do say so myself."

Jennifer was disappointed, and she glared at the shelves as if her need would miraculously create the book out of thin air. It wasn't the end of the world, but it would have made things a lot easier if—

"Well, well, well," Marysue whispered.

Jennifer looked where she was pointing and saw a thin blue pamphlet with *Thaler* printed on the spine. It was shoved between two books on the shelf below where they'd been searching. She took it out, turned it over, and saw that it was indeed about the academy.

"Freshmen," Marysue said as they rushed to the nearest table. "I told you they were jerks. They don't know how to file their own nails, much less a book."

Jennifer hushed her impatiently and began to read, trying not to squirm as her friend read over her shoulder.

It was obviously a privately printed work, detailing the history of the school from its inception to a period some ten years ago. From the amount of dust on the covers and paper, it was also obvious that no one had looked at it in years, if ever, and she suspected it had been a labor of love for some now forgotten professor.

"Fascinating stuff," Beauford said sarcastically when the last page was flipped over. "I'm thrilled by the plot. Rich boy meets greedy farmer, greedy farmer takes rich boy's money, and rich boy founds his own school so he can get richer and his kids can get a free education."

It was basically true.

And it was no help at all.

Jennifer closed the pamphlet wearily and rubbed at her eyes. Yeah, nice try, she thought, and squinted at Marysue when she saw her friend holding back a laugh.

"What's the matter?"

Marysue pointed. "You've just scrubbed thirty years of dirt onto your face. You look like a raccoon."

Jennifer wiped a sleeve over her face and returned the pamphlet to where it belonged. She checked the books again in case she'd missed something, checked them a second and a third time until her eyes watered with the effort.

Marysue called to her, then hurried down the narrow aisle and jerked her thumb over her shoulder. "Enough," she said. "Nancy Drew you're not, child, and hungry I am. Do you realize we haven't had lunch? So what do you say we blow this joint and get ourselves something fattening."

"I suppose."

Suddenly, Jennifer whirled around and ran back to the shelves, grabbed the pamphlet, and turned to the last page. "Here!" she said excitedly and held it up to the dim light. "Marysue, take a look at this!"

"Look at what?" Beauford asked, taking the pamphlet. "I don't see anything."

"Look again. Do you see?"

"I see, but I don't see. Why would someone cut out the last page?"

"I don't know," she said. "But if I'm right, it's the only page that has John Innlake's name on it."

Marysue started to ask a question, but the words turned into a strangled yell when someone turned out the lights.

Chapter Nine

FOR THE FIRST FEW SECONDS THERE WAS MIDNIGHT IN the library, until slender traces of light from around the edge of the heavy shades enabled them to see the far end of the aisle. Dimly. As if they were looking distantly through a fine black veil. Then, signaling each other unnecessarily to keep quiet, they dropped into crouches and waited, hoping to hear Esther's voice telling them she had changed her mind and wanted her keys back so she could close up herself.

They heard nothing.

There was only the strong smell of floor polish, the musty smell of books.

Maybe, Jennifer thought hopefully, it was only one of the security guards, making his rounds of the rooms that were supposed to be closed for the day; or maybe it was Mrs. Klopher, the head librarian, back to turn the lights off herself. It was something the woman would do—no one believed she trusted anyone under the age of fifty.

Jennifer refused to think it might be one of *them*.

It couldn't be—not in broad daylight, not here on campus with all these people around.

It couldn't be.

But they couldn't take the chance.

Marysue was ahead of her, bobbing nervously on her heels. Jennifer put a hand on her back and, when she turned, gestured to the right. Keeping low, they moved to the back wall and along it to around the next stack.

All they could see were the tables. The front of the vast room was dark.

The next stack, and another look, and on down the line toward the far wall. Barely breathing, freezing each time a floorboard creaked or a shoulder brushed against the bottom of a shade. They averted their eyes from the windows so as not to lose what little vision they had.

A chair scraped on the floor. Someone had bumped into it.

It was possible that whoever was in the room didn't even know they were there.

But it was just another possibility. Why would he turn off the lights to move around the room?

They still couldn't take the chance.

Jennifer pressed her hands against the outside of the stack and peered around it, taking a short breath when she saw a shadow dart around a table in the opposite direction.

Marysue was already at the last aisle, and from the position of her legs she was bracing herself for a run to the door. Jennifer crawled up behind her as quickly as she could, looking over her shoulder nervously until she heard the scrape of a chair at the far end of the room.

"Now!" she whispered harshly, and they lunged headlong up the aisle, using the wall to propel them along, not taking the time to look left when they burst into the study area and dodged around the tables, their eyes only on the faint light under the doors dead ahead.

The thud of several books tumbling to the floor.

Jennifer reached the doors first and charged through them with a slap of her palms, not looking back as she took the stairs down two and three at a time, feeling her palm burning as it slid down the metal banister. At the landing she nearly fell when she swung herself around the newel post, and nearly fell a second time when Marysue slammed into her back, rebounded, and passed her on the other side.

Then they were outside, the light blinding them, slowing them until they were moving at a fast walk toward their rooms.

Marysue was panting, and perspiration ran down her face. "I think," she gasped, "if it was Esther, I'll strangle her."

Jennifer nodded and gulped for air. "I'll be right behind you."

"I wasn't scared, you know."

"Sure."

Suddenly Marysue stopped and pointed rigidly at a group of girls playing with a Frisbee on the lawn. "Look at them!" she said angrily. "Just look at them! Don't they know what's going on around here?"

"No," Jennifer said calmly. She took the girl's arm and led her inside, straight up the stairs and into her room. She closed the door and leaned against it, listening for sounds of someone following.

Marysue sprawled on the bed. "I can't take this, Field. I'm not kidding. I really can't take this."

"I know, Marysue. Believe me, I know."

"We have to get Lee and Conrad, Jen. We have to get the guys."

She agreed. Whether it had been pride or just plain foolishness she didn't know, but trying to do this on her own wasn't going to work. She had to remember that she had friends, real friends, who were just as involved as she was.

And she shrieked and leaped for the chair when some-one knocked on the door.

"Nice," said Barbara when she poked her head in. "I just love getting screamed at when I call."

Jennifer, one hand on her chest to slow her heart, waved her other hand airily, and Marysue groaned and rolled over to face the wall.

"You guys drunk or what?" Barbara came in, looked around, and rolled her eyes toward the ceiling. "It smells like a locker room in here. You been jogging or what?"

Jennifer shifted without sitting up. "Yeah. We're into health today. What's up?"

"Health means showers, you know," O'Malley said. "Have you guys seen Monica around?"

Marysue hiccoughed.

Jennifer's face darkened. "Yes. A couple of hours ago. She nearly bit my head off for no reason."

"No kidding?" O'Malley's eyes brightened at the scent of gossip. But when Jennifer refused to elaborate, she shrugged and pulled at the side of her white T-shirt. "Well, if you see her, would you tell her I'm looking for her?"

"Sure," Jennifer said, and Marysue hiccoughed again.

Barbara closed one eye and looked at them both. "You're not drunk, right?"

"Barbara . . ."

"Okay, okay, I'm going, all right? Just let Monica know, okay? It's important."

The door closed, and Marysue rolled onto her back, her face red from holding in the laughter that now burst into the room. She grabbed the pillow and shoved it over her face, and Jennifer could only gape at her until she felt laughter of her own beginning to swell in her chest. It wasn't the time, but she couldn't hold it off, and before long they were both hooting and shrieking, mimicking Barbara's stance and voice until their strength ran out.

Finally, Marysue staggered to her feet and grabbed a handful of tissues from a box on the dresser. She dried her face, stared in the mirror, and said, "So that's what hysterics are, huh?"

"I think so," Jennifer said.

"I don't like them. Definitely a low-class emotion."

"Definitely," Jennifer agreed, pushing herself to her feet. "Now let's call Lee. Maybe we can meet the guys right away, maybe they're back from . . . wherever."

"Right," Marysue said, and she fished some change from her pocket. "I'll call. You get cleaned up. Then I'll get cleaned up while you decide what to do next."

"Me? Why do I have to decide?"

"Because," Marysue said with a wink, as she left, "you're Nancy Drew, not me."

"Thanks," she muttered to the closed door. She wrinkled her nose and thought, *so this is what fear smells like.*

The cold water felt great, and Jennifer splashed more on her face, swallowed some, and groped for the towel she'd draped over the basin. One more handful, and she looked in the mirror and saw her reflection frowning back at her.

Something at the back of her mind was trying to force its way out. Something important she had either seen or heard but could not get a grip on. Her eyes closed, and she waited, hoping that whatever it was would slip into her conscious thoughts. But she gave up after a few seconds, confident that it would make its appearance sooner or later.

When Marysue hadn't returned by the time she reached her room, she changed her shirt, retied her pony-tail, and decided she couldn't look more like a typical 1950s teenager if she tried. Straight out of all those old movies—except that in them everyone always lived happily ever after.

"Whoa!" she said then, backing away and glaring at herself. "What kind of attitude is that, huh?"

Marysue barged in, and Jennifer was glad she didn't jump, though her legs tensed and her arms felt like lead. She only picked up a pad and pen at Beauford's direction and followed her down the hall.

Most of the rooms were closed and locked.

One trapped music softly behind its door.

Jennifer hesitated at Monica's door, suddenly curious about why the girl would be so furious at her for dropping off the envelope. It occurred to her that it might be the wig; maybe Monica was really sensitive about it and was afraid Jennifer would blab it all over campus.

There was no way of knowing, and she wasn't about to hunt for her and ask. Monica had had her chance, and she'd blown it; compared to what was happening now, Monica's tantrum wasn't worth a single thought.

"Field," Marysue hissed, "you haven't got X-ray eyes, so come on."

"I—never mind."

She made it into Beauford's room just before the door slammed, and she dropped onto the bed. A glance around, and the only thing she could see that was different from her own place were the prints on the walls—horses, most of them horses, and all of those racing. And a sprig of long-dead magnolia in a bottle on the window sill.

She tapped the pad with the pen. "So? What am I supposed to do?"

"Make a list," Marysue ordered. "Like they do in mysteries. Write down everything we know about those . . . things, and anything else you can think of that might have something to do with them. Then we compare them and see what we come up with."

"If you know so much about it, why don't you do it?"

"Who, me?" Marysue turned around, washcloth in hand. "Why, child, I'm just a spoiled little Richmond girl without a brain in her sweet little ol' head. You got the smarts. You do the work."

Jennifer made a face at her.

"No, dear, that won't do," Marysue said as she walked out the door. "If you don't do it, I won't tell you what Lee said about you when I talked to him just now."

The door closed.

Jennifer raised her arm to throw the pen, looked up at her hand, and grinned. After a moment's thought she divided the first sheet in half with a line, labeled one side "Known" and the other side "Unknown." Then she began with as objective a description of the creatures as she could, added where she had seen them and whom they had attacked or possibly murdered, as in the case of John Innlake.

She left open the question of their connection with Thaler, though she noted the missing page at the end of the pamphlet.

She didn't describe the lab—just starting to do so had brought back too many horrid memories; she decided to fill all that in later.

By the time Marysue returned, Jennifer had jotted down the questions she had asked herself earlier about origins and purpose.

"Done?"

Jennifer nodded. "I think so." She handed over the pen and notebook. "See what you can add, okay?"

Marysue dropped them onto the dresser, and as she squirmed in and out of a bewildering variety of T-shirts and blouses, she read the pages aloud. When she was finished, both reading and deciding on a loose black T-shirt, she rubbed the pen thoughtfully against her cheek.

"I think I thought of something," she said, her tone questioning whether she ought to bring it up at all.

Jennifer tilted her head and waited while Marysue brought the end of the pen to her mouth and chewed on it, looked at it in disgust, and tossed it onto the bed.

"I think—"

But before the girl could say another word, Jennifer leaped up and shouted, "That's it!"

Marysue blinked. "What's it? I didn't say anything yet."

Jennifer picked up the pen. "This."

"What about it?"

"Last night, when Monica left, she was teasing me about being a detective. She said something about using a blackboard to make lists and things."

"Yeah, so?"

"She . . ." She passed a hand over her face. "We had to put it all down, she said. Including the pen."

"Yeah . . . oh."

Jennifer nodded. "Right. How did she know Dean Innlake was holding a pen when he died?"

Chapter Ten

"BUT YOU *MUST* HAVE SAID SOMETHING ABOUT IT!"

Jennifer, finding it hard to keep her voice down so no one would overhear them, trailed Marysue hurriedly down the stairs to the front door.

"I didn't. I can't be positive, but I'm pretty sure I didn't say anything."

On the porch they paused, somewhat surprised that the sun was so low in the sky until a check of their watches told them it was past five. There was muffled noise from the direction of the Student Union, and a quartet of helmeted bike riders was racing around the arc of the drive. Jennifer watched them until a wind gust made her shiver—the warmth of the day had already begun to fade, and the light jackets they carried seemed too flimsy to break the cool breeze that slipped down from the hills.

Finally Marysue started them moving again, off the porch and toward the parking lot, but Jennifer could barely see where she was going. The impact of what she had said upstairs was still strong enough to unnerve her, and she didn't want to follow the thought through.

Monica.

If Beauford was right—and Jennifer could not remember much of what had been said to the other girls in the hall—then Monica knew more about Innlake's murder than she'd let them think.

Much more.

In order to have known about the pen, she would have had to have been there. In the living room itself. And since, according to Detective Ives, Innlake had not been dead for more than an hour, she might even have been there during the murder.

No, she told herself. You can't think that. You can't. Monica was the one who showed you how to survive here, how to talk to the other girls, how not to feel so homesick every night. She had been a friend. A protector.

"Hey, Field, wake up!" Marysue said.

Jennifer blinked, brushed an annoying strand of hair from her eyes, and saw that they were already at the Thunderbird. Beauford was behind the wheel and turning the key over, grinning at her as she jumped in.

The engine ground, whined, but didn't catch.

They exchanged glances, and Marysue tried again, until a faint smell of gasoline filled the car.

"Nuts, I'll flood it," she said and sat back with a sigh. "Dumb old car."

"Maybe it's a sign."

"What?" Marysue rolled down her window. "Don't get weird on me, Jenny. If you do I won't tell you what Lee said."

"What?" she asked, trying not to seem too eager.

Beauford laughed. "Nothing."

"He wasn't home." She lifted a hand. "Really. I talked to his father. He said Lee went out, didn't say where he was going except that he'd probably eat at the Hilltop. He thought, he told me, he was going to see his girlfriend."

"Oh no. " Jennifer closed her eyes and smiled. "What about Zucco?"

"No answer there, either. And before you ask—no, I didn't try the Hilltop. Half the time the phone doesn't work, and the rest of the time no one bothers to answer."

A minute passed, and Marysue tried starting the car a third time. When that attempt failed, she slid out, muttering. Jennifer joined her as she lifted up the hood and looked in.

Jennifer gasped, and Marysue swore.

As many wires as could be reached had been yanked from their moorings, leaving a tangle that told them the Thunderbird was useless without the work of an experienced mechanic.

Beauford dropped the hood angrily, punched it with a fist, and whirled to stare at the buildings. "When I find out who . . ." Her shoulders sagged, and her head turned slowly from side to side.

Jennifer grabbed her hand and pulled her toward the drive.

"Hey, what are you doing?"

"Walking," she said. "We've got to see Lee and Zucco, we've just got to."

"But it's three and a half miles!" Beauford protested.

"Most of it's downhill."

"Who cares? Three and a half miles is not a stroll, you know. Our feet'll be worn to the bone! Hey, look, why don't we try to get a ride?"

"From who? Do you know who owns any of these cars?"

"Not really, no, but—"

"Then we walk. It's as simple as that."

"Field, you're not listening!"

Jennifer ignored her. The shadows from the dormitories, the Student Union, the classroom buildings were already darkening the lawn, and if they didn't start soon it would be night before they reached Staines. And she did not want to be on the road in the dark. She wanted houses and people and noise.

Marysue was resigned and suggested as they walked between the pillars that they might get lucky and be able to hitch a ride. A farmer could pass by, or someone heading into town to go to the movies. It was, after all, Saturday night. People around here had to do something on Saturday, didn't they?

Jennifer didn't respond, and she didn't remind Beauford that virtually no one lived north of the valley, not for miles. She slipped on her jacket and stuffed her hands into its shallow pockets, keeping her head down and watching her feet take the blacktop in easy strides. There was no sense walking on the graveled shoulder; any traffic that came on them from behind they would hear in advance.

Marysue whistled.

Jennifer tried to put Monica out of her mind, but in doing so she found herself staring at the shadows.

Shadows of trees that stretched like a black picket fence across the highway.

Shadows under the trees where small animals scurried and birds flew invisibly.

The brick wall that marked the academy's property was hidden by brush and tree trunks, and twenty minutes later it was as if they were walking an endless road through a wilderness that had never once seen a human being.

The breeze began to rise into a wind that bent the treetops, soughing and rising to a keening. Their footsteps were made louder by the mournful, lonely sound surrounding them.

"Field?"

"Yeah?"

"Do you wonder . . . I mean, have you ever thought about what these things might be?"

She nodded.

"I mean, I've been thinking, and I've decided they have to be mutants of some kind."

"Mutants?" Jennifer looked at Marysue, puzzled.

The road began a long curve to their left, putting their backs to the lowering sun.

"Yeah. Those experiments they were doing, maybe they were trying to get themselves back to normal. Maybe they're really people who got messed up somehow. I mean, when you think about it, what else can they be?"

The grumble of an engine sounded behind them, and Marysue turned to walk backward, her thumb out to hitch a ride. "What do you say?"

"I don't know what to think," Jennifer admitted. "I don't know much about mutants and things like that."

"Well, think about it, then. So far, it's the only answer we've got. Unless you want to tell me we're talking about werewolves."

An old black pickup, battered and streaked with rust, its bed piled high with bales of straw, appeared around the bend. They stopped and waited. Jennifer took her hands out of her pockets and smiled while Marysue waggled her thumb in case the driver didn't get the idea.

He didn't slow down. When he saw them, he swerved awkwardly to the middle of the road and sped by, not even looking in their direction. Bits of straw fluttered to the blacktop.

"Well, I'll . . ." Marysue glared at the truck and shook a fist at it until, three hundred yards farther on, it vanished around a second curve.

At that moment the road became too empty, too quiet, and the wind reached down to twist in their hair.

"Nice guy," Jennifer muttered.

"I have better words than that," Marysue said grumpily. "But southern ladies simply do not express their feelings in that manner."

They walked on. As they neared the next bend the road began to angle downward into the valley, gently, then steeply. The shadows deepened as the trees grew taller and crowded the shoulders as if trying to form a barrier across the highway. On their left now the land rose toward the top of the hill they were walking around and down, and on their right, beyond the shoulder, the land fell away sharply. The foliage was still too thick and high for them to see Staines, but they knew it was there, and they quickened their step.

And just before they reached the bend they heard something in the trees, on the hillside above them.

"What was that?" Marysue asked without stopping.

"I don't know."

It's probably just an animal, she thought. Just some kids playing, or a rock falling. That's all it is, just a falling rock.

It came again—something moving through the brush, just far enough up the slope to remain in the shadows.

Jennifer edged closer to the side of the road, glancing over her shoulder every few steps until it was clear that whatever was in there was pacing them, and moving down.

Without saying a word, Marysue broke into a trot, and Jennifer stayed with her.

The wind increased again, and the keening lowered to a grumbling as if a storm were approaching. Leaves spiraled out of the trees and scratched across the blacktop to tear at their ankles and slap against their legs. A crow wheeled overhead, cawing loudly before looping higher and vanishing.

The trot became a run.

Jennifer wanted to run as fast as her legs would take her, but the road grew steeper as they reached the bend, and it was all she could do just to keep her balance.

Marysue dropped behind, panting and holding her stomach, gasping for Jennifer not to get too far ahead.

She slowed as the curve straightened and grinned in spite of the stitch in her side when she glimpsed Staines down below and the patchwork spread of the farmland on the other side. A more beautiful sight she could not imagine, and she felt herself smiling. Then a look over her shoulder to see if Marysue was all right, and she stumbled sideways to a halt.

Something dark and large had left the cover of the woods and had darted across the road to their side and behind them. Twilight was just upon them, and Jennifer couldn't see it very clearly; nevertheless, she knew.

It was close.

Very close.

We're not going to make it, she thought as Marysue turned to look as well; we're not going to make it.

"It's one of them, isn't it? It's the first one I've seen," Beauford said, licking at her dry lips and gulping for air.

"I don't know."

They ran on, slower now, their legs weighted, their feet feeling every pebble and crack in the road.

Abruptly, Jennifer's mind cleared, and she knew they would never reach the first house at the bottom of the hill. Despite the slope, they were too tired; fear had drained their strength. She slowed.

"Conrad's," she said. "It's closest."

Marysue saw where she was looking, nodded, and at a silent signal they veered sharply off the blacktop and plunged into the trees, not bothering to find a common path since they both knew where they had to end up once they reached bottom.

Branches jutted out at Jennifer's eye level, damp leaves on the ground made the footing treacherous, and roots hidden beneath those leaves threatened to trip her. The angle of the slope here was far steeper than that on the road, but she took most of it sideways, her run more a slide and push now, using a trunk to shove her onward, using a large rock to slow her momentum.

She heard Marysue, somewhere below and to her left.

She heard something else, to her right and not far away, a crashing as though whoever was chasing them had given up all thought of stealth.

A thorn bush forced her to move left.

A rotting log in her path was too large to go around, so she jumped it, landed neatly, and raced on, following what she imagined was a deer trail—a narrow, almost clear lane that seemed to be taking the easiest, if not the swiftest, way down.

Another thicket, and she didn't think twice about swinging around it without slowing.

But the land dropped off sharply into a dry creek bed, and there was nothing she could hang on to. She fell, landed a third of the way from the bottom, and rolled, arms flailing until she reached level ground. There her head struck a thick dead branch, and she rolled to a stop, unconscious.

Chapter Eleven

WITH A MOAN THAT ESCAPED BEFORE SHE COULD STOP it, Jennifer awoke suddenly and nearly cried out again when fireworks blossomed somewhere deep in her skull. She held her breath against them, prayed for them to leave her, and when it was dark again she sighed and didn't care who heard.

Her eyelids fluttered then. Needles jabbed at her neck, her hands, her left arm where the jacket's sleeve had been shoved up to the elbow. And a knife stabbed at the back of her head until she realized it was only the place where she had struck the branch.

Her eyes opened.

It was dark; a fragment of the moon winked at her through the wind-tossed leaves.

And the ground was cold and damp beneath her, causing her teeth to chatter until she clamped her jaw shut tightly.

I'm alive, she thought. I'm alive.

How long she had been unconscious was impossible to determine, but she knew that she didn't dare stay in one place for much longer. She moved carefully, testing her limbs to be sure nothing was broken, sobbing silently at the throbbing in her head. She thought at first she was imprisoned in a cage of some kind, and fighting off a

panic that dried her throat and filled her mouth with
sand, she used her right hand to probe the darkness
around her, pushing, grasping, realizing at last she was
tangled in a branch's many arms.

Safe again, and still alive.

She lowered her head onto her arm and rested, taking
deep breaths, hoping her night vision would at least permit her to see a few yards, if not more. And as she did she
felt moisture on her cheek. Blood, she thought; oh no,
I'm bleeding. Her free hand touched her skin timidly, a
finger went to her mouth, and she licked it, preparing to
gag. It was water. She looked up and saw that the moon
was hazy, seeming to float through a cloud.

Fog. It was only fog.

Then she remembered what had happened, and she
froze. And listened. But there was nothing out there as
far as she could tell. Only the wind, and the fog, and the
rasp of her breathing.

After waiting for what she guessed was five minutes,
she began to crawl away from the branch, freezing each
time a twig snapped or a piece of bark fell, until at last
she was free. A turn onto her back, and she leaned against
the slope, so steep she was almost sitting upright. Then
she prodded her head gingerly, wincing when her fingers
found a tender, egg-sized lump. But here, too, there didn't
seem to be any blood, and already the ache was subsiding
to a dull and persistent roar.

The wind died.

The moon dropped slants of silver through a gap
between two massive trees.

Within moments she was able to see where she was—
the creek bed, the steep walls, the lumps and piles of forest debris she had brought down with her in her fall—and
decided that the darkness and the branch had been her

allies, hiding her from whoever had chased her until, apparently, he had given up. At least he hadn't been able to run any faster than she had.

Unless, she thought with a start and a silent gasp, he had caught Marysue.

A tear instantly fell from one eye, and she brushed it away angrily with the back of a hand. There was no time for that. She had to get up, get moving, find someone to help her find her friend before it was too late.

Her legs wouldn't respond when she willed them to move, and she slapped at them, cursed them until they were able to support her. Pinpricks of light danced behind her eyes; the headache threatened to explode out of her skull. She stood for a long time, swaying, before shuffling and stumbling off to her left. The best thing to do, she thought, would be to continue on down the slope. It wasn't that far to the bottom; if she didn't fall and break a leg or her neck, she ought to make it in only a few minutes.

And when an unseen branch snapped under her heel, she decided there was no sense trying to be quiet. She was still too dizzy, and despite the moon it was too dark. If someone was out there waiting, there was nothing she could do about it. She would have to take her chances.

She stuck to the creek. Though it wandered and would take more time, it was the only sure way of reaching her destination without smashing into trees or falling into depressions that would snare her.

The wind rose and fell; the moon climbed and became brighter.

And finally she saw a light ahead. A steady light. It was a lamp in someone's window.

Jennifer sobbed with relief and moved faster, leaving the creek when its banks became level with the land around it, stumbling through the brush until she had to stop for a rest, so her head would cease its pounding and her dizziness would pass.

A hand wearily wiped the perspiration from her face, and she blinked rapidly to bring her vision back into focus.

And she looked at the light again and couldn't believe it.

It was moving.

It had seemed steady before because she was moving toward it, but once she stopped it was clear it was a large electric lantern being carried. Now, without fear to distort her thinking, she could see that it bobbed up and down, swung side to side; and when she listened hard enough she could hear footsteps and low voices.

Then a flashlight switched on, its beam slashing past the trees to land on her face.

Run! she ordered but had no strength left. The best she could do was stumble a few steps before her legs gave out and she fell onto her back.

The footsteps ran toward her.

The white beams darted above the ground fog, touching a bush here and a large boulder there, finally sweeping over her legs and returning, to hold them when someone shouted, "There!"

Her hands scrambled for something to grab—a stick, a rock, anything she could use as a weapon as she pushed herself up on her elbows and began a frantic backward crawl.

"There! Over there!"

The roaring in her head increased again, and she was deafened by it, her eyes filling with tears of pain.

"Dammit, Jenny, stop moving so I can find you!"

And a moment later someone was straddling her legs, and the flashlight aimed upward.

"Boo," said Lee Fawkes, and Jennifer fainted.

When she came to a second time she was lying on a large bed, still dressed but covered with a light blanket. Marysue was sitting on the mattress beside her, and Lee was in the doorway, hands thrust into his pockets. He was scowling, and his cheeks were red. When she sat up, he only looked for a moment before leaving, closing the door behind him.

"Drink," said Marysue, handing her a glass of water.

She did, and it tasted wonderful, and when her free hand went to her head she found a bandage wrapped around it. The bump still ached, but not as forcefully, and her skin felt as if it had recently been washed.

"You okay?"

She nodded slightly. "I think I'll live. Where are we?"

"Zucco's. This is his mother's room. When I got here I made Lee and Zucco go after you." Her hair was a mess, and she pushed at it feebly. "I think they thought we had scared ourselves. They didn't believe me right away."

"How long have I been out?" She glanced at her watch, but the crystal was broken and one of the hands was missing.

"It's almost eight. Mrs. Chang isn't here; she went out to dinner."

Jennifer nodded again, testing her head, then looked to the door. "What's the matter with Lee?"

Marysue wouldn't meet her gaze.

"Beauford, what?"

"I yelled at him for scaring you," Marysue said contritely. "I know I shouldn't have, but I was so scared when I saw you lying there that I couldn't help it. I'm sorry. Really."

"He'll get over it." And with a sigh she shoved the blanket to one side and swung her legs over. Then she grabbed the other girl's shoulders in a hug and a silent thank-you before pushing herself to her feet.

"The Fields make 'em strong."

A knock on the door had Marysue on her feet as well, and she opened it to let Conrad in.

"If you're feeling better," he said, "I think you ought to come see what Lee and I discovered."

Jennifer looked at Marysue and followed them into a long hall, to a doorway and steps that led up into the attic, which had been transformed into a combination bedroom and workshop. At the back was the bed and other furniture, separated from the rest by a high Chinese folding screen. And the rest was impressive.

There were work benches, a few woodworking tools on shelves, cabinets, a word processor, and at the front a telescope aimed out a large round window. On the finished walls were NASA photographs of the planets and artists' renditions of galaxies, stars, and planets that existed only in their imaginations. Lee and Conrad were standing at a large table just in front of the telescope, and they were watching her carefully.

Marysue grinned. "He's going to be Luke Skywalker when he grows up." And when Conrad actually blushed a little, she laughed. "Actually, he likes Darth Vader. He's not as dull."

Lee moved away from the table and walked toward her, concern narrowing his eyes until she let him know with a smile that she was all right, that she wasn't about to drop into another faint.

"Sony I did that," he whispered as he brought her to the table. "I didn't know you were hurt."

She squeezed his arm and relaxed when an answering smile brought a light to his eyes. Then she looked at the table and saw a series of what looked like maps of constellations Conrad had taken from magazines or had drawn on his own. They were divided into grids, and each square held a number of large and small white dots next to which were lettering and digits she couldn't read.

She shrugged. "I don't get it. These are stars, I guess, but I don't understand the rest."

Conrad leaned over and pointed to each of the papers. "These are star charts, Jenny. Like maps of the sky. Every star we can see has a name and a number that's registered so an astronomer in France can talk about a star to an astronomer in India, and they'll both know which one they're talking about."

He turned to a desk behind him and picked up a sheet of paper. "And this is what Lee found in Dean Innlake's study the night he was killed." He placed it on a clear space in the middle of the table. "When you look at it now, you can see right away it's a star chart. He must have copied it from a book."

Jennifer saw the similarities but not the purpose. "So why did he circle that one at the bottom, and that one over there?"

The room grew quiet.

Deep within the house she heard the grumble of a furnace.

Conrad wiped his hands on his jeans, cleared his throat again, and pointed. "This one, here at the bottom, is the sun."

Jennifer's eyebrows lifted.

"And this one is Alpha Centauri. It's a star a lot like ours, the scientists figure, and they're almost positive it has planets revolving around it, just like our sun."

"All right," she said and frowned. "So?"

"So . . . I think, Jenny, Dean Innlake discovered something about that star, and that's why he died."

Jennifer looked from face to face, looked down at the chart, and suddenly straightened up. "No," she said.

"Yes," Conrad insisted. "Jenny, after everything you all have told me, I'm convinced that Mr. Innlake thought these creatures of yours are aliens."

She turned away, stood beside the telescope, and stared out at the sky. "What about you?" she asked quietly.

"I don't have a better answer," Conrad said. "I think he was right."

Chapter Twelve

THROUGH THE TELESCOPE, THE OCTOBER MOON WAS close enough for Jennifer to touch. Somewhere on that barren gray landscape men had landed, had walked, had done experiments, and had taken samples; somewhere on that lifeless satellite astronauts in clumsy-looking space-suits had shattered forever the wall that had prevented man from leaving his home planet.

They might not walk there soon again, but the wall was down.

So why, she thought, was it so difficult for her to believe that other races on other planets had also shattered their walls? Why was it so hard to imagine that beings that may or may not look like humans could travel the distances between the stars, could for whatever reason land here on earth?

Nothing lived on the moon.

Nothing lived on Mars.

Except for man, nothing at all lived in the entire solar system.

She supposed that if explorers, real or mechanical, had discovered other life forms, it wouldn't be hard at all to accept Conrad's theory. But they hadn't, and it was, and when she turned back to the room the others were watching.

"I'd almost rather believe in werewolves," she said in a small voice.

Then she reached for a ladder-back wooden chair that leaned against the wall and sat down heavily. Her hands were clasped tightly in her lap, and she stared at the dozens of small scratches she saw there, the results of her fall into the creek bed. They were real. If she hit them, pulled the skin around them, they would sting, maybe even bleed.

But aliens?

"How did they get here?" she asked Conrad. "What do they want? What are they doing? Where are they from?"

"I don't know," he replied gravely. "And I'm only guessing about Alpha Centauri. It could be almost anywhere out there. Pick a star, though it makes more sense that they'd come from someplace nearby." A quick grin. "Nearby, that is, in terms of space travel, not driving to New York."

"What do they breathe, then?"

He scratched at his head for a second. "Air, I guess."

"Whose?" Marysue asked. "Ours or theirs?"

"Well, it has to be ours, right? I mean, we haven't seen them walking around with tanks on their backs. They'd stick out like sore thumbs, and there's certainly no scuba diving around here."

"We have no proof," Jennifer said then. "For all of this, we don't have any proof."

Lee nodded. "And we'll have to get it, or no one will believe us. The question is—how? We don't even know who they are."

"Innlake," said Marysue after a long second of silence. "He must have known something, isn't that what you said? Maybe in his house there's . . . oh." She stopped and put a finger to her mouth, and her eyes widened as she realized what she was proposing.

"What about your friend, the cop?" Jennifer said when Lee came over and sat on the floor beside her chair.

"Larry Ives? You've got to be kidding."

"Why?"

"Because he's a cop! He uses facts and evidence, Jen, not fairy stories from a bunch of kids. And that's why he's going to think, you know—it's a bedtime story, or a movie we saw. He's not going to believe us. He'll think it's a joke, and he won't think it's very funny."

And as they brought up and discarded other possibilities, Jennifer knew that he was right. No one would believe them, not the authorities, not their parents, and certainly no one at either of their schools. In fact, she still wasn't sure she believed it herself, though the more she thought about it the more it seemed to make the most sense ... if anything about it made sense at all.

Conrad gathered up the charts and put them neatly on a shelf. Then he perched on the table and swung his legs back and forth. "You know," he said, "one of the problems is people."

"People?" Marysue asked.

"Sure. It's so hard for an ordinary person to imagine life in outer space that he decides it doesn't exist. We're the only ones around, and that's that, no arguments." He gestured toward the telescope, the pictures, the piles of charts. "You see, it doesn't make any difference that we can't even begin to count the number of stars out there, or begin to know how many of them have planets. It doesn't make any difference. We're special, he thinks. What he doesn't realize is that that means we're alone."

Jennifer stared at him in admiration, amazed once again that behind that large frame and innocent face was a brain that never seemed to stop thinking. And wondering. And looking for answers.

Lee drew his legs up and clasped his hands around his knees. "Well," he said, "as one poor earthling who has seen these things in action, I think I'd rather be alone."

"I myself am not an admirer of philosophy," Marysue said in her best Virginia accent. "So if y'all don't mind, could we please stick to the subject?"

"Which is?" Conrad asked.

"Which is, my dear, now that we know what we know, what are we going to do about it? I myself am in favor of heading straight for the nearest jungle and hiding out until the invasion is over."

"We don't know it's an invasion," he protested.

"Yes, we do," Lee argued without raising his voice. "Maybe not with spaceships and *Star Wars* weapons, but if they came here as friends, they sure don't know how to act like it."

Jennifer stared into her lap.

"They've killed people," he continued. "And we know why—because they don't want us to know about them. Mr. Innlake is a good example, if we're right."

"So," Jennifer said, "we'll have to do what Marysue said."

"Who, me?"

She nodded. "We'll have to go to Innlake's and take a look around."

They decided to leave right away, before Conrad's mother came home and they found themselves making excuses they knew would only sound feeble. But once on the street, they were in no hurry to walk into town. The night, once a time they enjoyed, was no longer theirs. And not one of them looked up to see how many stars were visible over the valley, stars that were being slowly erased by drifting, filmy clouds.

Conrad and Marysue were almost a full block ahead when Jennifer took Lee's arm and held it close to her side. "I'm scared," she said, leaning her cheek briefly against his jacket. "I'm real scared. Are you?"

"To death," he admitted.

"I'm still not sure. Are you, Lee? Are you really sure?"

He nodded. "I don't need that proof. What we saw in that lab, and what we saw in the park . . . yes. It wasn't a costume I saw. I believe it because . . . because I believe it."

Jennifer shivered when a dog barked, jumped when a cat dashed out from under a hedge and across the street. "And you don't think we're crazy?"

"Oh, sure, we're crazy. I'm a regular loon, don't you know that?"

Her smile was wan.

"But I still believe it."

She moved even closer, and soon he slipped his arm around her waist, forcing her to match her stride with his. And she didn't say another word on the long walk to Innlake's street; then she stopped and stared back toward the center of town.

"What?" Lee said anxiously. "Someone following us?"

She shook her head.

"Then what? What is it, Jen?"

Marysue and Conrad ran back to them, and it was a while before Jennifer was able to remind Beauford of something she had said earlier that day.

Monica and the pen.

Lee and Conrad looked at each other, and Conrad momentarily covered his eyes with one hand.

"Jen," Lee said, "are you saying she's one of them?"

green eyes in a dream

"No, don't be silly. She can't be. But if she knew about the pen, maybe she knows . . . what we know now. Maybe she's working for them."

"Holt?" Marysue said in clear disbelief.

green eyes, watching

Once again, Jennifer was positive she was missing something important, but she couldn't put her finger on it. It was more than Monica's abrupt turnaround, and more than the fact that she knew about the pen. Something . . . something . . .

She shook her head. "Forget it for now," she said briskly. "We have to get going before someone sees us and thinks we're going to rob them."

Lee hesitated as if he wanted to argue, then led them on up the street, walking past the Innlake house as if it wasn't their destination. Then he took them around the block, to the house just behind. Luckily it was dark, and he ran across the lawn to the backyard. There was a hedge separating the two properties, and, after wasting a minute hunting for a natural break, he forced one himself.

They waited in the darkness, listening for sounds that would betray someone watching, or a neighbor coming out to a back porch. But their luck held, and they ran in a crouch to the back stoop, where Lee opened a screen door and grabbed the inner doorknob.

"Locked!" he whispered.

Marysue immediately jumped down and tried each of the windows along the back, shook her head, and rejoined them.

Jennifer pressed close to the house, knowing that at any minute someone was going to glance out a window and see them, or a patrol car was going to drift by, just to check on things.

Then Lee pulled out his wallet, took out a plastic-coated driver's license, and within seconds jimmied the lock. He opened the door quickly and herded them all in, closed and locked it behind them, and let out a breath he'd been holding since he started.

"How did you know how to do that?" Jennifer asked in a voice only he could hear.

He grinned. "I watch a lot of TV." And he grinned again because he knew she didn't quite believe him.

They were in a small, old-fashioned kitchen, and with Conrad in the lead they made their way cautiously toward the front, using the faint glow of the streetlamps to guide them until they reached the study.

"I don't suppose anyone brought a flashlight," Marysue said.

Conrad patted her on the head and pulled a penlight from his shirt pocket as he directed her to pull the shades on the window behind the desk. Once they were sure no one would see them from the outside, Marysue was stationed in the doorway to watch the street and warn them in case they had to make an escape.

The folders, books, and papers were still piled on the floor and chairs, just as they had last seen them. And after some stumbling indecision, they began at the desk. Quickly. Trying to remember where things were so they could be replaced.

Fifteen minutes later Jennifer was ready to give up. They had found nothing but old term papers from Innlake's teaching days, record books, letters to and from a sister in Missouri, photographs of Innlake with his faculty at the academy, and some unreadable notes he had taken on what she gathered was a book he was writing about some obscure Middle European king.

Nothing about the star chart.

Nothing about the wolves.

They tried the books on the shelves, hoping to find something stuck between the pages; they tried looking under the desk, under the rug, behind the paintings on the walls, even for envelopes taped under the desk drawers; they flipped through every one of the folders.

Again, there was nothing.

Then Marysue hissed and ran into the room. "Someone's coming," she warned.

"Who, the cops?" Lee asked.

"I don't know. I didn't see anyone on the street, but someone just tried the front door."

Jennifer felt her stomach lurch and grow hollow when Conrad switched off the penlight. She had to swallow a scream when Lee took her arm and led her to a doorway she hadn't noticed in the lefthand wall. When Conrad nodded, Lee opened it, and she saw a flight of worn wooden steps leading down into the basement. It was the only place to hide; anyone coming in now would find them in a second.

Marysue hissed again and waved them on impatiently as she stared into the next room.

Lee nodded, and Jennifer held her breath as she followed him down, wincing at every creak of the stairs, checking behind her at each step to be sure the others were coming. At the bottom Conrad used the light again.

There was nothing unusual that she could see—the furnace, piles of junk, a broken chair, spider webs, spider eggs, and a thin layer of dust on an uneven concrete floor. It even smelled like a cellar—age and dirt and things forgotten by time.

She hugged herself against the damp chill that clung to the walls in spite of the furnace, and followed the others quickly as they made their way around the staircase to hide in back. There was an uncovered lightbulb hanging from a thin wire, but they didn't dare turn it on in case someone saw a glow under the door.

Lee discovered a small, empty closet under the stairs, but it was too shallow to hide them all. He was about to dismiss it when they froze at the sound of a footstep directly above them. With a brusque wave Lee ordered Marysue and Jennifer in, gave them both a wink, and left the door open just enough for them to see out. Then he and Conrad vanished, the penlight extinguished, leaving them alone and in the dark.

Please, Jennifer prayed. Please don't let them find us.

Marysue had a tight hold of her arm, but she didn't pull away. It was painful, but it was contact.

Then the cellar door opened, and light spilled into the closet from cracks between the stairs.

Chapter Thirteen

JENNIFER LOWERED HERSELF INTO A CROUCH, PULLING Marysue with her until they were huddled against the closet's damp back wall. Beauford was trembling, and when Jennifer nudged her in a gesture of comfort, she shook even harder and closed her eyes.

Jennifer shifted, grimacing in anticipation of making a noise that would give them all away. The closet was makeshift, a hastily built storage area that took advantage of the space beneath the staircase. It would offer them very little protection if someone was determined to get in.

She held her breath and closed her eyes tightly.

She felt a spray of dust on her neck when the footsteps moved down cautiously. It felt too much like a spider walking across her skin, and it was all she could do to keep herself from wriggling.

Suddenly Marysue jabbed her and pointed mutely at the open door. Jennifer swallowed, reached out, and took hold of the knob.

The footsteps continued down, stopping again at the bottom.

She pulled the door closed but couldn't release the knob; if she did, the click of the bolt would alert the unknown searcher, and she was forced to inch forward and grab the knob with both hands. If whoever it was tried the door, maybe he'd think it was locked; and if he didn't, she and Marysue would be able to make enough noise to get Lee and Conrad to their aid.

She hoped.

A hope that faded when the doorknob moved a fraction of an inch toward her. She eased her hold and knew when it moved again that it wouldn't be long before it came off.

A grunt as the searcher barked his shin on the broken chair.

Jennifer lowered her head. She hadn't heard him move; once off the stairs, he was completely silent, and now she wouldn't know where he was, how close he was to her.

A shuffling as feet scuffled across the floor.

Then he reached the door.

She heard him out there, breathing slowly, and she bit down hard on her lip when she felt a hand grip the doorknob on the other side. Her arms trembled; perspiration ran onto her brow, down her sides; and a cramp began to build in the arch of her right foot.

She needed to breathe, but she didn't dare. The slightest sound, the slightest move . . .

A tug on the knob.

She bit her lips against a scream but held on.

Another tug, a bit harder. A kick on the door that rattled the doorknob and almost tore it loose from Jennifer's hands. "Damn." Through the door the muttering voice was barely loud enough to make out the words. "Have to come back with a crowbar." And suddenly he walked away to the stairs, paused, then ran up and slammed the cellar door.

Jennifer didn't move.

It might be a trick, she cautioned herself. He might still be up there, waiting.

There was a muffled thud, and she frowned. That might have been the front door, but how could she be sure? The searcher might have left, but he might also have let someone else in.

At last the cramp grew too painful to bear, she had to stand, or scream. Wincing, she rose in agonizingly slow stages, trying not to lose her grip as she did, praying that Marysue wouldn't say anything, wouldn't try to help.

Suddenly the doorknob came off, and she was thrown backward into Beauford and the plank wall. She yelled, and the door was thrown open, a spear of light stabbed in her eyes, and Conrad said, "Hey, you trying to tell the whole town we're here?"

Marysue instantly bolted into Conrad's arms with a muffled cry. Lee took the penlight and knelt beside Jennifer, who was trying to stand up.

"Are you hurt?"

"No," she said, dusting at her hair, her arms. "I may be dead from fright, but I'm not hurt." She looked up then. "Is he gone?"

Lee nodded.

She let him pull her to her feet and started to knock the dust off her shins when she saw something near the juncture of the back wall and the concrete floor.

"Lee, point the light over here."

"What's up?"

She gestured impatiently while she repeated the order, and he poked his arm over her shoulder, not arguing when she took hold of his wrist and aimed the light where she wanted.

"Hey," he whispered excitedly.

The wall's center plank had been knocked in by her fall, and what had caught her eye was something pale behind it. She pushed at it with a finger. It was paper. Pushing the plank in a bit more, she reached in and pulled it out.

"What is it?"

"I don't know," she said.

"Do you think it's Innlake's?"

"It's his house."

It was a package about six inches square and tied together by cord. In the circle of the narrow beam she saw that the top page had been torn from a book, or . . . She gasped and looked closer, and recognized the Thaler Academy pamphlet with its cover ripped off.

Holding the prize in one hand, she groped in the empty space to see if anything else had been secreted there; all she found was dust and rotted wood.

"Well?" Lee said.

Quickly, she scrambled to her feet and pushed him out of the closet ahead of her. She went to show the package to the others, but Conrad demanded they leave the house then, before whoever had been there returned. He and Lee had ducked behind a pair of overturned workbenches, and neither was able to tell her who the searcher had been.

"He just looked around and left," Conrad said. "And that's exactly what we're going to do. Split, before we get nailed."

Caution prevented them from running, but they moved as swiftly as they could, back up the stairs and out the kitchen door. They charged across the backyard and through the gap in the hedge, ran to the street, and headed for town. Jennifer wanted to stop, to look at what she was carrying, but the others' urgency was too strong to fight, and she went with them, glad now for the lights in the houses, the streetlamps, the sound of traffic ahead.

The cellar's chill hadn't left her, and she didn't think it would for a long time.

Once on the main street, noting that the clouds had thickened and there was a hint of rain in the air, they voted against going to Conrad's house. The Hilltop was closer, it had people in it, and there was enough noise there to cover whatever conversation they would have. And they were hungry—the excitement, and the fear, had stimulated their appetites, and Jennifer realized that she and Marysue hadn't eaten since breakfast.

But once they were in the back booth, the jukebox blaring, her appetite fled. She thought about the closet, the footsteps, and the chill became a cold that made her grip the edges of the package so tightly her fingers began to ache.

She didn't hear the waitress take their orders, nor did she blink when Lee glanced up at the clock and announced that it was only after ten when it ought to have been dawn. But she did feel his hand gentle on her shoulder, and when she looked at him she smiled at the concern in his eyes.

"Are you sure you weren't hurt?"

"Yes," she said. And took a deep breath. "I just keep trying to tell myself this isn't a dream, that we're really here."

Conrad poked a spoon at the packet. "Well, are we going to open it or what?"

"Open it," she said, and picked up her knife to saw the cord away. When it was done, she divided the packet into four sections and handed them out, examined her own, and found pages torn from notebooks, from magazines, and from books, all of them marked with Innlake's scrawl.

The food and drink came and was forgotten.

The theater's late show ended, and the luncheonette was packed with adults and kids demanding immediate service.

Finally, Jennifer sat back and rubbed her eyes wearily with her knuckles. The others were just as quiet, picking at their food though it was cold now and tasteless, ignoring calls and comments that came their way. Conrad emptied his glass of soda at what looked like a single swallow. When he put the glass down, he shook himself violently. The burp that followed was so loud, and so crude, that they stared at him before Marysue began to giggle, Jennifer laughed, and Lee reached across the table to lightly punch his arm.

"All right," Jennifer said, "let's see what we have."

"What we have is the proof," Lee told her. He was solemn, and his face was emotionless. "I didn't want to know it, not really, but this is the proof."

They pooled what they had read, swapping papers back and forth, pointing, reading aloud. When they were done it was well past eleven, and Jennifer knew that Lee had been right.

Innlake had known them.

There was no indication whether he had met the wolf creatures by accident or if they had come to him, but he had known them and he had worked with them. No reasons were given, though Lee suspected bitterly the association had continued because they'd threatened him, not because he was thrilled at the opportunity to work with visitors from another world.

It was Innlake who had purchased the laboratory equipment the girls had discovered; it was he who had assisted the aliens in setting up the lab itself, though he didn't say anywhere what it was all for—except to note in one place that without it the wolf creatures were sure to die.

"He was wrong there," Conrad said glumly.

"We don't know that," Jennifer said. "Maybe the one that's left will die, eventually."

"Die of what?" Marysue asked.

"I don't know," she said sadly. "I just don't know, and I wouldn't know how to begin guessing."

They were further frustrated because there were no names mentioned, either alien or human, as if Innlake were afraid his notes would fall into the wrong hands. Nor did he say how many of them there were. After some discussion, Jennifer and Lee provided the number. Four, they reasoned: the three who died and the one who had attacked them.

"If there were more," Lee said, "we'd know it."

They also found a star chart, one far more sophisticated than the one Lee had discovered in the study. It was this that proved Conrad right in his guess about their original home, though Innlake kept referring to it as "Wolf Star." And on a sheet of paper attached to the chart was a time line that none of them believed when they first saw it.

"It's impossible, that's all," Marysue said emphatically.

"Why?" asked Conrad.

"Because, that's why."

"That's no answer. That's a kid's answer."

She grabbed the sheet up and waved it like a flag. "But if it's true, it means they didn't just come here, don't you understand that? It means they've been here for . . . for years!"

"Off and on," Conrad said, squinting at the notations. "It means they've been here for centuries."

"But why?" Lee asked, confusion making his voice too loud.

Werewolves, Jennifer thought with sudden excitement; I'll bet this is where the werewolf legend comes from. Some poor old man or woman or some little kid sees one of them taking off the disguise and becoming what looks like a wolf that walks on two legs. They wouldn't know about stars and planets, they'd only know about ghosts and vampires. A man who changes into a beast isn't an alien, he's a werewolf.

"I don't know," Conrad admitted. "But it looks like they came and went just like they were going to work or something, like this was their office." He slapped a palm on the pile of papers in front of him. "I wish we had more! I wish we had the whole story, not just bits and pieces! It makes me want to scream!"

Jennifer took up the time line and the notes that went with it and stared at them again. Conrad, she decided, was probably right—the earlier visitations were frequent but they didn't last long. But if Innlake's own speculations were accurate, this time they had come to stay because they'd already been here for a decade, if not more.

But without the lab, they would all die.

All—how many?

Die—of what? Did the lab provide them with inoculations against disease, with immunity against earth's bacteria, with means to—

Jennifer looked at Conrad. "At your house we were talking about what they breathed."

"Huh?"

"You know, you said they'd have to breathe our air."

He looked puzzled. "Right. I mean, if they didn't, they'd keel over in the street, right?"

"No," she said quietly. "No, they wouldn't."

And a voice said, "Incredible. You found it, and I didn't. You certainly saved me a whole lot of work."

They said nothing. They only looked up, directly into the eyes of their hunter.

Chapter Fourteen

"YOU DON'T DARE DO A THING," LEE SAID. "NOT WITH all these people around."

"That doesn't bother me," the alien said with a friendly smile. "What are you going to do, tell them I'm from outer space and I'm holding you prisoner?" The alien laughed and shook its head. "You know, I really don't think you understand what you've gotten into."

"We know all right," Lee answered. "And we know that you killed Dean Innlake."

The alien's eyes widened for a brief second before its lips curled into a sneering grin. "Well, well, you're smarter than I thought. Congratulations again. But you still don't get it."

"Then explain it," he said flatly. "I'm really stupid, you know. Really stupid."

"Don't push it, Fawkes," the alien warned. "Don't push it."

Jennifer took Lee's hand and gave him a slight push. "Go," she said grimly.

"I wouldn't if I were you," the alien warned.

"Like he said," Jennifer whispered loudly, "you don't dare try to stop us."

For the first time, the alien seemed uncertain.

"And if you do try something," she continued, "you wouldn't like it if I clawed your face off."

Marysue held Conrad's hand and slid out of the booth. Lee, hesitating until he was poked again, followed them, and Jennifer scooped up the papers and tucked them under her arm.

She was trembling.

Her heart raced so fast she thought it would explode in her chest, but she slid along the seat, stood, and nearly screamed when the alien took hold of her arm.

"I'll be following you," it said.

"Follow us all you want," she replied. "It won't get you anywhere."

"You're a fool."

She hurried toward the exit, feeling as if she were walking through one of her nightmares. The luncheonette seemed to double in length, and the voices around her were muffled, as if she were listening to them underwater. Her knees weakened, and she forced them to lock, so that by the time she reached the door she was virtually stiff-legged, awkward, and the arm that pinned the papers to her side began to protest.

"You're making a mistake."

Refusing to look around, she stepped out onto the side-walk and saw Lee waiting for her a few yards up the street at the curb. The alien was right behind her, matching her step for step until she stopped and whirled around.

Whatever she was going to say, however, was trapped in her throat when she saw the gun pointing at her stomach.

"These things come in awfully handy," said Larry Ives. "Especially when people think you're a cop."

"I trusted you," Lee said angrily.

"A lot of people did," said Ives. "I guess they were wrong." He slipped the gun back into his jacket pocket, but he made it clear it was still aimed at Jennifer. "Now that's my car over there, the green one. I think we all ought to go for a ride."

"Where?" Marysue asked fearfully.

The alien only smiled, winked at her, and urged her on with a wave of his hand.

Lee lifted his fists as if ready to attack, but Jennifer shook her head quickly. His hands dropped, his shoulders slumped, and when they reached the car Conrad opened the door.

"I think," Ives said then, "you'd better drive, Miss Field. Your boyfriend here might think it clever to try some-thing if I had the wheel. And," he added when she turned to protest, "don't tell me you don't drive. I'm not so sure I'd believe you."

"But I don't!" she said, blinking to keep her eyes from filling with tears. "I really don't."

Ives stared at her, finally nodded, and motioned with his free hand for Marysue to take the wheel. She opened her mouth to argue but knew it wouldn't do any good. Ives had already seen her in the Thunderbird. And an obvious lie now would be more than just foolish—it could very well be deadly.

Jennifer, Lee, and Conrad were crammed into the backseat, while Marysue slid in behind the wheel. Only then did Ives take his place on the passenger side, sitting with his back against the door so he could watch Beauford and, at the same time, make sure the others could still see the gun.

"Where to?" Marysue asked.

"Out of town, Miss Beauford. Go out toward your school."

Marysue was nervous and stalled the car twice before the engine ran properly. Then she pulled out into the street and headed for the hill. She drove slowly and every so often wiped a hand over her face and back through her hair.

Jennifer watched her and wished there was something she could do to help. But Lee, sitting in the middle, was hunched over and fuming, his rage creating an almost tangible heat that made the car too warm, too close. Conrad sat rigidly with his back straight and his hands in his lap. She had the feeling that if she touched him now he would scream.

"What are you going to do with us?" she asked when the silence grew too long.

"I'm working on it," Ives said pleasantly. "You'll be happy to know, though, that I Can't kill you." Marysue whimpered and stared at him in panic, and the car swerved onto the shoulder before she could bring it back under control. "Oh dear, Miss Beauford, please watch where you're going, if you don't mind. You know very well I can't kill you. Not all four of you. Too many questions, even for a cop to answer. No, I'm going to have to think of something else."

"But why the school?" Jennifer wanted to know.

"Why not?"

"But the other kids, the teachers . . ."

Ives's face was hideous in the green glow of the dashboard lights, and worse when he turned to her and showed her his teeth. "Miss Field, if you've read these papers you already know the answer to that."

And she did.

One of the first things she had read was the missing last page of the academy history pamphlet. It was a listing of previous deans and the names of all the trustees. Until ten years before, when the number of trustees had been abruptly reduced to one—Peter Dramon. Either he was one of them, then, or at the least working with them as Innlake had done, and had somehow managed to get complete control of the school, and therefore its facilities.

Her hand covered her mouth.

"I see you begin to understand at last," Ives said.

She couldn't nod, but she knew he could see it in her eyes.

A spray of raindrops spattered the windshield, and Marysue groaned softly as she flicked on the wipers. She looked at the detective, then over her shoulder at Jennifer, who sank back in her seat and jammed an elbow in Lee's side.

"I think you'd better let someone else drive," she said as the land began to rise and the hill was black before them.

Ives shook his head. "It's only a brief shower, my dear. I don't think our Miss Beauford will have any trouble."

"But she will," Jennifer insisted. "She hates driving in the rain. She almost killed us a few weeks ago, isn't that right, Lee? She doesn't know how to handle—"

"Enough!" Ives snapped, bringing the gun up to point at her head. "I'm not—"

"A maniac," Conrad said, his voice hinting of fear. "She panics, you know? She has this thing about rain, something—"

"I said enough!"

Marysue pushed back in the seat until her arms were almost straight. The rain was falling steadily now, just enough to coat the windshield, but not enough to let the wipers clear it off without squeaking.

And with the town behind them, there was nothing ahead but the white slash of the headlamps, silver darts of rain, and the gleaming black road. The forest on either side was an ebony wall once in a while flaring into gray when the headlights swung into slight curves and illuminated the leaves bouncing in the wind.

Suddenly a deer ran across the road, its eyes reflecting red in the headlamps. Marysue screamed and slammed on the brakes, and the car skidded to the right, spat gravel up from the shoulder, and would have plowed into a tree had she not regained control again and brought them back to the tarmac.

"I can't do it," she said, taking her foot from the accelerator.

"It was only an animal," Ives told her, and he placed the gun against her head. "You will drive, Miss Beauford, or I will change my mind."

Jennifer saw a tear on Marysue's cheek, and she looked at Conrad and Lee, their faces in shadow. From Lee's position, she knew he was still angry, but now he was back in control.

"Please," she begged as they reached the first sweeping curve in the middle of the hill. "Please, let her come back here and let Lee drive."

Ives didn't turn his head. "No."

"Hey, come on," Conrad pleaded. "If you don't kill us, she will."

"He's right, Larry," Lee said, too calmly.

Jennifer spoke again, and Conrad did as well, and together with Marysue's genuine weeping they filled the car with an unholy noise that soon made Ives swear and swing his gun hand over the seat, the weapon's muzzle less than two feet from Jennifer's eyes.

"One more word," he said. "One more word and—"

Marysue screamed, and the car sped up suddenly, veering sharply toward the verge. Ives was thrown into her shoulder, and at the same time both boys leaped for his arm, Lee putting an elbow into his chin while Conrad grabbed his wrist and twisted the gun toward the roof.

It went off like a cannon in the enclosed space, and went off a second time as Ives struggled to pull away. But he was pinned to the back of the seat by Lee's weight, and hampered still further when Jennifer began punching him on the head, on the back of the neck, anyplace she could reach, while Marysue swung the car back and forth.

Ives's arm bent upward.

The gun fired a third time, the bullet smashing the driver's window and making Marysue throw one hand to her head in feeble protection. Then she shouted a warning, but it was too late.

Jennifer had just enough time to see the trees grow impossibly large before branches scraped across the roof and the glass, before the tires jounced over a rock, before the car slammed into a cage of white birch, and everything went black.

"I smell gas!" Conrad yelled as he pushed open his door and pulled Lee out behind him.

Jennifer, shaking off the daze that followed the crash, hurried out her own side, opened the passenger door, and grabbed Ives's arm. "Help me," she gasped when his body refused to budge.

"Why?" Conrad asked, his arm around Marysue as he led her toward the road.

"Evidence," Lee said groggily. He staggered around the car and took the man's other arm.

Together, fighting against the explosion they knew would come, they tried to pull the detective free, but the dashboard and a section of the engine was jammed against his chest. To move him was impossible.

Then, as Jennifer backed away, his head turned and his eyes opened.

His lips moved.

She didn't see any blood.

"Jenny, come on!" Lee urged, taking hold of her arm.

"No, wait a minute," she said, and with a shudder she reached over Ives to take the papers from the seat where they had dropped.

He spoke.

Jennifer, despite her fear and Lee's rising panic, stared at him. "I can't hear you," she said, while at the corner of her vision she saw a flickering flame reach toward the seat from under the steering wheel.

"Nice . . . try."

She put a hand to her cheek to keep her head from trembling. "I don't know what you mean."

The flame came closer, close enough to his face almost to lick the false skin. The mask bubbled and cracked and started to peel away, revealing sleek fur.

Ives grinned. "I'm dead. No more trouble. Right?"

He reached up, wincing from the effort, and clawed the remains of the disguise from his face, revealing the wolflike features of her nightmares. For an instant Jennifer saw on his right side a red ugly patch.

"Jenny!"

He coughed, and his eyes closed slowly.

Jennifer knew she had to leave, and she knew she had to stay, too, to listen. And when his lips moved again she only looked at him blankly and did not resist when Lee finally grabbed her shoulders and virtually carried her away.

When the gas tank exploded, she barely felt the wave of hot air, barely heard the fire, barely saw the world turn orange, red, and white.

"Jenny?" Lee said anxiously. "Jenny?"

"Later," she said dully. "There's something else we have to do."

Chapter Fifteen

THEY HUDDLED IN THE SOFT RAIN AGAINST THE DORMITORY wall. The fire exit was open, and Conrad was balking.

"This is crazy!" he protested. "If we get caught, we'll be sent up for life!"

Jennifer wanted to laugh; instead, she glared. "We have no choice. Don't you get it, Zucco? We don't have a choice!"

Conrad looked uneasily at the building. "I don't know. Maybe there's another way."

Jennifer wanted to grab him, shake him, but she only took his hand and held it tightly for a moment. "There is no other way. You know that as well as I."

"Yeah," he said at last. "I suppose."

"There's no supposing about it. I told you what I saw. I told you what Ives said, didn't I?"

"He could have been lying," Marysue said softly.

"No," she answered. "He wasn't. He wanted me— us— to know that we shouldn't think we've won." She paused, remembering the words so harsh in her ear. "He wasn't the last one. Well, I know who it is, and we're going in there, now, and we're going to end it once and for all."

They had walked around the building twice; all the lights were out, and there were no sounds from

inside—no music, no talking, nothing that would indi-
cate anyone was still awake. But Conrad, incredibly,
couldn't bring himself to go inside the girls' dorm, not
until Marysue finally took hold of his hand and yanked
him across the threshold. Then she slapped a hand over
his mouth and warned him with a look not to say a word.

Jennifer led the way.

At the second floor, she checked the hall carefully
before hurrying toward her corner room. She made sure
the door was unlocked in case they had to duck inside,
then led the others past her door, and knocked on another one. Her free hand lightly covered the doorknob, and
she tried to turn it.

It didn't move.

She prayed, don't let it be locked.

She tried again.

On the third try she felt the knob turn. Without wasting a moment, she put her shoulder to the door and
pushed in, the others right behind her.

Someone switched on the light.

Monica Holt opened her mouth to scream, but Lee was
behind her, holding a hand over her mouth while Conrad
pinned her arms to her sides. Then Jennifer pointed to
the closet, and Marysue grabbed the bathrobe that hung
from an outside hook.

"Hold this in front of her," Jennifer said.

Monica's eyes widened, and she tried to kick free, but
the boys' grip was too strong, and she was unable to stop
Jennifer from taking hold of the side of her nightgown
and ripping it down to the waist. Immediately Marysue
wrapped the robe as best she could around her, save for
the side where Jennifer stared at the patch.

"Breathing," she said.

"What?" Lee asked.

"Breathing. That . . . that thing there helps them breathe our air. We were talking about it at Zucco's, remember? And I saw something like it on Ives. And I remembered a tank or something at the secret lab. One of them went inside, and I'll bet that's where they went when they needed a larger dose of whatever it is they breathe."

Conrad grinned. "Y'know, I think she has something there!"

"But how?" Marysue said.

"There are medicinal patches," Conrad said, "that have doses of certain kinds of drugs in them. You put them on, and they seep through the skin directly into the bloodstream. But how did you figure it out, Jen? I mean—"

Monica kicked out again, pushing hard off the floor and dumping the three of them onto the bed. She almost escaped, but Lee managed to keep his hand over her mouth, and Conrad quickly pinned her arms down again.

"Poison ivy," Jennifer said. "She told me she had poison ivy just like Barbara. But then I saw the patch in the shower room, and it was more than just gauze. It was red, like it is now." She paused and matched Monica's infuriated stare. "Later on, I bumped into her on the stairs. Just bumped, and I hit her side, and she acted like I had punched her in the stomach . . . like I had knocked all the wind out of her for a second.

"It's the patch. It's how they live when they have to walk among us."

And she reached out toward it, ignoring the girl's sudden frantic squirming, grabbed the tape that held the four-inch-square patch in place, and yanked it off.

Monica screamed and bit down on Lee's hand. He swore, but the damage was done. She jerked away from him, snapped out from under Conrad, and stood in the center of the room, panting, perspiring, holding the robe in front of her like a shield.

"What the hell are you talking about?" she demanded.

"Knock it off, Holt," Marysue said. "We know who you are. Or we know *what* you are."

Monica gaped at them all. "You're all nuts! You're all crazy. I'm going to call security and—"

Marysue moved to stand in front of the door. Lee and Conrad got to their feet, and without touching her they moved her over until she dropped into her chair.

"How long?" Jennifer asked. "How long before you suffocate?"

Tears formed in Monica's eyes, and she looked blindly from side to side as her hands danced over her chest, the arms of the chair, finally lighting against her stomach.

"I don't know what you're talking about," she said in a small voice. "I don't, I swear it."

"How long?" Jennifer insisted, and pointed at her side.

Monica's eyes cleared then. "The patch?" She squirmed and bared her side. "Is this what you're talking about, Field? Is this what's making you so damned crazy?"

Lee looked away, but Conrad couldn't help staring. "Oh no," he said. "Oh no, Jen."

There, midway up Monica's side, was a T-shaped incision, barely healed and still showing the pock marks where stitches had been taken out. There were already signs of the scar that would remain when the healing was done.

"A cyst," Monica said between clenched teeth. "A cyst, Field. They took out a cyst!"

Jennifer didn't know what to say. She felt her mouth working like a fish's gasping for air, but the words wouldn't come. After Ives, after Innlake, she had been so *sure*, and had been so *wrong*. A sob broke then, and she whirled around, pushed Marysue to one side, and opened the door to run back to her room. She didn't want to see anyone, talk to anyone, and it was like hitting a glass wall when she reached the threshold and stopped.

And in less tune than it took her to take a step back, she remembered what she had been trying to bring to mind since she'd gotten out of the woods.

She and Marysue, standing outside, watching O'Malley run back into the dorm.

And Marysue had said "*Poison ivy? I thought she could roll in it and not catch a thing.*"

And Barbara O'Malley was suddenly beside her, saying, "Well, don't just stand there, Field. Aren't you going to ask me in?"

Jennifer stepped to one side numbly, watching as the redhead walked into the room, frowned at Lee and Conrad, and grinned at the state of Monica's undress.

"Hey, what's this?" she said. "A party?"

But Jennifer wasn't listening.

She backed into the hallway with a slow shake of her head, pressed herself against the opposite wall when O'Malley turned around and grinned again.

With her lips, but not with her eyes.

Not with the eyes that shone a faint green.

"Lee," she gasped and put a hand to her mouth when other doors opened, and other girls came out, and she saw the dead smiles and the dead glow of their eyes.

How many are there, she thought. How many *are* there?